To Nancy,

Wonderful to see you at the Conference! Hope to see you at the next one, too...

Best Wishes, Frankie

FatLand

a novel

Frannie Zellman

PEARLSONG PRESS
NASHVILLE, TN

Pearlsong Press
P.O. Box 58065
Nashville, TN 37205
www.pearlsong.com

ISBN-10: 1597190152
ISBN-13: 9781597190152

Cover & book design by Zelda Pudding

Quantity discounts are available to your business, institution or organization for reselling, gifts, fundraising or educational purposes, or incentives. For more information contact
Pearlsong Press • P.O. Box 58065 • Nashville, TN 37205
615-356-5188 • sales@pearlsong.com

Library of Congress Cataloging-in-Publication Data

Zellman, Frannie, 1954–
FatLand : a novel / Frannie Zellman.
    p. cm.
ISBN 978-1-59719-015-2 (original trade pbk. : alk. paper)
1. Overweight persons—Fiction. I. Title. II. Title: Fat land.
PS3626.E38F38 2009
813'.6—dc22
                              2008037188

To the members of the Fat Underground

Prologue

2010

THE CENTER FOR HEALTH MATTERS recommends that any woman of childbearing age, defined as the years from 18–50, whether or not she intends to get pregnant, adhere to the following recommendations:

- No alcohol
- No premarital sex
- No weight gain
- No unhealthy foods in large quantities
- Foreign travel only for business purposes and for stays of less than three weeks...

excerpt from Surgeon General's Committee
Recommendations on Health & Weight

2012

THE CENTER FOR HEALTH MATTERS recommends that a series of Pro-Health Laws be passed according to CHM guidelines. Recommendations for food intake and weight categories follow.

- Every person who is considered overweight according to these guidelines must begin a reduced-calorie regimen immediately or risk mandatory enrollment in a Pro-Health Re-education Program if he or she has not seen a health professional.

- Every person who consumes more than the allowed daily or weekly portion of certain foods risks mandatory enrollment in a Pro-Health Re-education Center.

- Every person who avoids or tries to avoid the Non-Approved Food Tax while buying or ordering the foods specified below, which are taxable according to the Non-Approved Food Tax Statutes, is subject to mandatory confinement in a Pro-Health Re-education Center.

- No person who is over the allowed weight limits is to be considered healthy, even if he or she meets the requirements of any or all other criteria for overall and comprehensive health according to tests and evaluations...

excerpt from Surgeon General's Committee
Recommendations on Health & Weight

2014

I CAN'T STAND IT ANYMORE.

I am fat. I am not a criminal. I am not ashamed of being fat. I am tired of wondering when the doctors are going to order me to have so-called "corrective surgery'" that not only does not correct, but makes me sicker in the name of making me healthy.

Worse yet, I don't want my children to worry about their weights. I want them to be happy and healthy, whatever their body types happen to be. I don't want them to have to worry about everything that goes into their mouths. I don't want them to face bullying and harassment or, even worse, the shattering of their dreams.

We are tired of being mistreated and mocked and having our self-esteem taken away from us, tired of being considered criminals when all we did was to have bodies that metabolize food differently than thin people.

If you wish to join us, please call or email the following for more information...

post on FatHelp Blog:
A Blog for the Fat Community of the USA

2044
FatLand

Part I

Chapter 1

Joann & Reevie

JOANN AND REEVIE sat in a sunny kitchen with yellow walls and a porcelain plate under a rooster clock. Joann poured coffee into two Wedgewood cups and they leaned back.

"I don't know what to do," Joann said, sipping judiciously at the Brazilian blend. Her long black hair cascaded down pale plump shoulders just visible under the light green print of her robe. "It's keeping me up nights, but I didn't want to worry Ed. I have to turn in this financial report tomorrow, and he has to finish those soil tests. But it all seems—" She bit her lip and tried, fairly successfully, not to cry. "Okay, this is the problem. Mira—well, she just doesn't seem to gain weight."

"Is she eating?" Reevie asked, setting her cup down. Her almond-colored eyes, several shades lighter than her rich brown skin, gave her the look of a pampered cat. She stretched slightly in her seat, her round breasts and belly shifting as she raised her firm thick arms.

"Of course. She eats even more than Jesse, and he's filled out quite nicely."

"Well, look at it this way," Reevie said. "There are kids, and adults, too, who remain thin all their lives. We can't help it. They can't help it. It's not as if she doesn't get enough to eat."

"But it's so embarrassing, " Joann said. "I'm so afraid her classmates will start making fun of her. And she's already having trouble getting clothes. Even today her Phys Ed teacher asked her if she could speak with us. And another teacher asked her if both of her parents came from here, from FatLand. She was so angry. She said to him, 'My parents have been here longer than you have.' It's lucky the principal is an old friend of Ed's from high school, or it might have been worse." She bit her lip again. "What did I do? Why is my child so thin? Reevie, where did I go wrong?"

"You didn't go wrong anywhere," Reevie said, taking Joann's hand across the table and squeezing it. "Mira happens to be thin. It could be any number of things. But none of them have anything to do with you."

Reevie sighed as she left Joann's house and walked the six blocks to her own spacious Cape Cod. She could understand Joann's worries, although she didn't have the same problem with her own children, Aimee and Jenna. They were both lovely, voluptuous—a bit spoiled, yes, but totally engaging. Aimee wanted to major in dance therapy, while Jenna wanted to go into theater arts. *Another achievement of FatLand,* she thought, and one of the reasons she'd moved here—no field was off-limits to anyone because of his or her size.

She remembered how it had been for her when she had been a drama major at a well-known university on the "Other Side," as FatLanders called the country adjoining FatLand on its eastern borders.

First her professors had laughed. One well-meaning instructor had urged her to take up smoking to lose weight. Another one had given her a lecture on why "heavy" black women would never make it in the theater or on TV or in the movies. Especially in the movies. And now what did she see? At least one movie a month featured a substantial black woman—*fat,* yes, *fat,* she reminded herself. You were supposed to use the word "fat" in FatLand. Not in bitterness, not in pride, but to describe what you were, and what the great majority of the inhabitants were.

We are fat. Say it, Reevie. Say it simply. Say it for all the times you were told to starve and they called it a diet. Say it for all the times someone told you—some man, since she was straight—*that he loved you, but if you would just lose thirty pounds...*

Then again, there were the men who took her to bed and loved it, but wouldn't speak to her the next day.

She remembered how she had argued with her husband twenty years ago before she had been able to convince him to move to the brand new territory called FATLAND, which stood for Fat Acceptance Territory Lease Accession Non Dated. (The correct name would have been

Fat Acceptance Territory Lease In Perpetuity, but that first Governing Board perceived correctly that people might not be wild about living in a place called FATLIP).

Her husband, a general practitioner at the time, had married her quite selfishly because, as he told her two dates after they met, "You make me feel as if I could fly and I want to lean against your breasts forever." He admitted to buddies that he liked "big women," and since he was far and away the most successful of his friends, they didn't tease him about his preferences.

It was when Aimee, the first of their girls, was born and started to become adorably chubby that FatLand came into existence. Founded in the second decade of the twenty-first century with twenty-four couples and twenty proud singles, FatLand had mushroomed into a country-state of 400,000, with growth of 20 percent in its past four years. It stood to become a million-person entity in the next five years, maybe sooner.

She and Alvin moved here when Jenna came along. Even her husband had noted the increase in fat-baiting and fat-hatred at the same time that more Americans were becoming fat and yet living longer. It was as if the fat-baiters refused to accept that they had been fed a diet of lies about fat people by the media and still clung to their desperate need to scapegoat some group.

Ironically, in the media on the other side, fat people—especially women, for some reason—started to appear regularly. A culture war was being fought between those who felt that fat people did not need regulating and those who felt they needed to reduce their body sizes "for their own good."

Then, of course, the Pro-Health Laws had begun.

From being apathetic on fat issues her husband had quickly become a staunch activist, so much so that he was now one of the two medical representatives on the Governing Board of FatLand.

Chapter 2

Ava

As THE SUN STARTED TO SINK DOWN behind Furst Mountain and the hills leading to it, Ava breathed in the cool, crisp air, then let it out in a sigh of pure content. *Marcy,* she thought, *you should be here.*

Ava had just gone skiing. Her round red cheeks set off her bright dark eyes. She hugged herself from sheer happiness and from cold. She would not have dared to go skiing on the "other side."

Then she thought of Marcy. Again. Was it abnormal to veer so sharply and quickly from happiness to despair and back again? And to keep remembering someone for so many years? The heart took its own time to mourn, but—Marcy, her best friend and lover, had died from complications of weight loss surgery two years before FatLand had been initiated. Ava remembered, even now, trying to talk her out of it They had been sitting in her apartment at lunch, and she remembered to this day the lights in Marcy's opaque green eyes and her shining dark auburn hair.

"Marcy, you can't mean it! Why do you need weight loss surgery? We go dancing every week and you do drumming! You hardly ever get sick! You're healthier than I am!"

"But according to the charts, I'm 150 pounds overweight. Why should I have to drag all that extra fat around?"

"Marcy, over *whose* weight? And overweight for what? You dance so well. You're a great drummer. Why do you have to conform to anyone else's expectations of what your weight should be? I love you whatever you weigh, and you know that!"

"But if I got any heavier, you'd have to drag me out on a stretcher.

And what if I got sick? No hospital would take me."

"But we arranged for you to be covered under my insurance. Don't you remember?"

"Ava, I'm tired of worrying about being a burden to you. I'm going to do it, and that's that. Don't try to talk me out of it."

She still remembered how Marcy had looked after the surgery. Ava reassured her that she looked great, then ran out of the hospital to cry by herself in their bedroom, praying for the first time in 20 years. "Please God, Goddess, forces, let my Marcy live. Let her recover from this. Let us get through this somehow. See, I'll even go to Temple if she gets better and stronger."

And Fate seemed at first to make Marcy better as she celebrated her first weight loss in ages. "Look, Ava, look!" She pointed to the figure on the scale. "I'll weigh even less than you do soon."

Ava had laughed and put her arms around Marcy carefully to avoid the tubes. "As long as you feel good, I don't mind in the least."

Then one night she'd awakened for no particular reason to find Marcy slumped over the floor in the bathroom near the bathtub. A call to 911 had followed, with Marcy back in the hospital for a week while they ran tests. Turned out that the operation had not been done well and some stitches had ruptured. A surgeon who had not even met her until that moment sewed the stitches back into place. Incorrectly, it turned out. They had to rush her to the hospital again a week later, only to have Marcy's original surgeon castigate her for not sticking to her diet. When Ava had pointed out that he hadn't been available to resew the stitches after having botched them in the first place, he told her that he would only talk with Marcy from then on.

Two weeks after that, when Marcy started not to feel well again, Ava had said, "I know you'll get angry with me, but I think you should have it undone."

"You're just jealous," Marcy said.

"I don't want anything to happen to you," she replied.

Three weeks later Marcy had fallen while trying to get to the toilet in a hurry, hitting her head on the bathtub. The new stitches had ruptured. By the time they got her to the hospital again she was barely breathing.

They hooked her up to the monitors. Ava watched the lines waver, then become straight. She didn't need the nurses running into the room to tell her what had happened. She'd kissed Marcy's forehead and held her hand as the doctor—not the surgeon, luckily—had entered and told her quietly and with some compassion that there was nothing they could do.

Ava had not had a relationship since then, with a man or woman. At 49 she was a respected reporter for *The FatLand Free News* and put almost all of her energy into her job. She smiled and kidded around at times with her colleagues, but made friends only with one of them, the editor. The skiing trip was an assignment, the kind of "look-how-healthy-we-FatLanders-are" piece that ran with increasing—and disturbing, to her mind—frequency in the "FatLand Life" column.

She had to admit to herself that she had loved the feeling as her skis had carried her down Furst Mountain, the smiling instructor waving her down and giving a thumbs-up sign as she brought herself to a stop. But the assignment was also the paper's peace offering to several members of the Board who were pushing for better relations with the Other Side, even in the midst of the Pro-Health Laws.

Every time she thought of Marcy and what she had gone through, and how she had died so unnecessarily, Ava felt a sour taste in her mouth at the idea of normalization. She didn't want FatLand to be on "normal" terms with a country that promoted weight loss surgery so constantly and vigorously.

Chapter 3

Alvin

ALONE IN THE STUDY—he refused to call it an office, old-fashioned as he was in some matters—Alvin read the minutes of the last meeting of the Board while he listened with half an ear to the conversation going on in the large, welcoming kitchen, his favorite room in the house. He and Reevie had purchased the huge butcher slab table and the high wooden chairs and cushions, as well as the copper kettles and pans hanging on hooks, a week after they had moved into FatLand. They had both exulted in the fact that they no longer had to feel guilty about welcoming people into their kitchen and cooking up huge, wonderful meals, the kind that left you dreamily content and on the edge of falling asleep with a smile on your face.

But now the Board was discussing an issue that would abruptly nip that feeling of contentment and pleasure in the bud.

For the very first time since its founding, FatLand, which had had a mortality rate just slightly higher than the "Other Side" for the last twenty-three years, had actually lowered its mortality rate. According to the latest reports, FatLand inhabitants were now *less* likely to die earlier than their Other Side counterparts, even with—or perhaps because of—the Pro-Health Laws.

He looked at the report again. The rates seemed to extend to all age groups, infants and extremely old people included.

Not exactly rocket science, Alvin thought, that if you give fat people insurance and have the government pay for it, if you pay for coverage of their children and don't discourage people from coming to the doctor by telling them they need to lose weight every time they come, people are more likely to receive the care they need, whether they are fat or not.

But of course that was not how the Other Side saw it. He scanned the headlines of the Other Side papers he read every day, some online, some through personal post.

FATLAND A HEALTH MECCA?
NEW STUDY HAS FATS LIVING LONGER

FATLAND UPS THEIRS:
MORTALITY RATES SPIRAL DOWN,
LEAVE DOCTORS WONDERING.

FATLAND FITLAND?
DO CHUBBOS HAVE IT OVER US,
OR IS SOMETHING ROTTEN IN TENT CITY?

FATS TRIUMPHANT:
STUDY TRUMPETS THEY LIVE LONGER, BUT HOW?

WOULD YOU RATHER BE FAT?
YOU MIGHT LIVE LONGER IN FATLAND

As he read the headlines and skimmed the accompanying articles, Alvin thought of the stormy Board meeting that had taken place that very evening. Harris, one of the owners of one of the biggest FatLand banks, had said, "It is our solemn duty to make sure that those results are correct and legitimate and then to repeat them next time. With that end in mind, FatLand National Bank will pay for memberships for anyone who wishes to participate in FatLand's GymNotTrim program."

"Why the hell do we have to send everyone to GymNotTrim programs?" Susan Weller, chair of the Nutrition Program at FatLand Greater University, had asked. "You know as well as we do that not everyone likes or needs to 'exercise.' On the Other Side they push everyone to exercise and diet, especially fat people, whether they want to or need to or not. Not only does it make some of them fatter, but it turns them off to exercising. Then they starve them, and yet a lot of them still don't lose weight. People here exercise if they feel like it. For one thing, it's a lot easier to walk if no one is calling you 'fat pig' or 'fatso' or 'tent girl' all the time. And there are sports leagues at all the gyms, including GymNotTrim. If FatLand National Bank wants to fund subscriptions for people who are there now, that's very generous, and I am sure GymNotTrim will appreciate it. But I don't like the idea of pushing people to exercise if they don't want to."

"Look," Sandor Forman, CEO of GymNotTrim, had said, "do you know what we would lose if it turned out that the results from the study could not be duplicated?"

"Since the great majority of your customers come from FatLand, I would say not a whole lot," Alvin had answered him. "They don't care what the study shows. You provide them with a place to exercise and have fun at a low cost, which is something they could never get on the Other Side."

"The problem is that we won't be able to provide those low costs a lot longer if we don't expand," Forman had said. "And that means going into the Other Side."

"So you think that if FatLanders happen to have a slightly *higher* mortality rate next time, the Other Siders will laugh at you and at FatLand?"

"We don't care about the laughing," Forman said, "but we do not wish to be seen as illegitimate."

"An ugly word, 'illegitimate,'" Margaret Clancy from *The FatLand Free News* said. "I haven't heard that word in all the time I've been here. Here a few agencies provide health coverage, so our mothers don't have to abandon their kids. Or they choose to get them adopted if they wish, and there are always people to take them. Aren't you selling your own services short by letting the fears of what others might say in some hypothetical instance influence you?"

"We've never had these results before," Harris said. "It would look mighty bad if they turned out to be temporary or worse, false."

"But why should they be false?" Alvin argued, wishing that his medical colleague Dara Simon, the other medical representative on the Board, were there to support him. "The methodology of this study was quite sound. Even in all the papers, they didn't fault it once. They were flabbergasted, but they didn't attack it. I think you're going overboard." *And pushing something that will have way more negative consequences than you understand,* he thought, but did not say.

Alvin looked out of the study window. Two years ago he and Reevie had planted phlox and geraniums near the borders of the slate and brick path leading to the pool. They both loved working outside. Good for the heart, he told her that spring, smiling, as they fanned their faces and inspected the places they had filled with seeds and hope.

Most of us already get exercise, damn it, he thought. Just not the showy kind that Harris and Forman think is "real" exercise. He hated the idea of forcing FatLanders to exercise, but even worse, to think that they had to exercise more or differently than they were already doing.

So many FatLanders took pleasure in walking around their communities, walking to the shops, walking in their yards or outside their buildings. There was no one to harass them here. Anyone caught harassing any FatLander was simply shown the gates—the first time. Second time meant permanent barring. It was that simple. Third time—there had never been a third time in his memory, but he believed the third time meant three years of community service in FatLand and a fine of one hundred thousand dollars. He grinned. Maybe the harassers were so ashamed at the thought of living among the people they harassed that they stopped after the second offense. More likely, he thought, they simply found other targets.

Alvin had always been what others thought of as big. He had never been called "fat," probably because at 6'4" and a heavily muscled 320, potential namecallers realized they would probably get a look at the pavement sooner than at Alvin's face if they let fly with negative verbiage. Reevie called his skin "chocolate cherry." He loved his work and the pleasures that his home, his wife and his kids brought him. He even sang when he examined people, causing some to smile and some to sing along. His patients adored him.

Telling FatLanders to exercise more or differently or both went against everything he believed not only about the health of fat people, but about health in general.

Health was not something to be pushed for in fear with others looking over your shoulder as you achieved one "goal" after another. Health was something you came by as you simply lived your life doing things you liked and being with people you liked. The less stress and worry, the less likelihood that your blood pressure would soar.

No one, he thought, but no one knew when someone else would

die, or what they would die of. And that went for fat people and thin people and all people. Doctors, especially, could not play God and tell others how long they would live and how they would die. Their task was to make it easier to live whatever years people had in good health, feeling positive about life and their bodies and themselves, however their bodies were shaped. Whatever caused FatLand's mortality rate to go down was probably at least partly a result of this philosophy, which was practiced by all FatLand doctors, not just Dara and himself.

And now the corporate types were panicking because FatLand had become better at letting people live, especially fat people, who had been told so much of their lives on the Other Side that they were doomed to live shorter lives because they were fat. And the changes they wanted to put in place would do exactly that if implemented, he thought—cause people to worry unnecessarily about their health and stress them and cause FatLand's mortality rate to go up once more...

Was What that what Harris and Forman wanted? The thought shocked him at first, then started his heart pumping faster and his brain grinding as it analyzed the evidence.

"Reevie," he said as she stepped into the study, "I have to meet with Dara as soon as possible. Would you like to come along?"

Chapter 4

Joann

JOANN WOKE UP TO THE HEADLINE in the morning edition of *FatLand Free News* over coffee and croissants. Mira, she observed, was eating nothing as usual, although she was drinking a cup of coffee without creamer or sugar.

"Board members split over offer from Bank: Bank to fund free Gym-NotTrim subscriptions for all in Fatland"

She shuddered. Mira was already exercising too much as it was. When she wasn't in her room lying on the bed and listening to music on headphones, she was running or working out on the biking machine. On the other hand, if this was some kind of rebellion, if Mira did see that the bank was funding free subscriptions, would it cause her to stop rebelling?

"Mira," she said to her daughter, who was staring listlessly at the table, "did you see this headline?"

"What headline?" Mira asked, tracing invisible designs on the white Formica table.

"The one about the subscriptions. For GymNotTrim. Funded by the bank."

"Oh, yeah?" Mira's eyebrows edged up. "Why are they doing that?"

"They want to give everyone in FatLand the chance to use the gym."

Mira reached for the paper. *Thank God,* Joann thought. *At least something still interests her.* Joann watched as Mira read not only the headline but the story beneath. When she was finished, she handed the paper to Joann.

"See you later," she said and stood up.

"You going upstairs?" Joann asked.

"Nope."

"Then?"

"Out."

Probably to do more running, Joann thought, her heart sinking again. Ed, of course, had left two hours ago. All of a sudden Joann realized that Mira hardly got to see her father these days. She wondered if that had anything to do with Mira's behavior or even her thinness.

She remembered how elated she and Ed had felt upon reading of FatLand's founding all those years ago, and how they signed up immediately, which of course was one of the reasons the soil testing contract had gone to him.

No harassment, they figured. No authoritarian doctors ordering them to lose weight. No worrying that they would be discriminated against at their jobs. No anxieties over what their children might think of them as fat parents. How ironic that her thin daughter seemed to harass them both by her stony silence.

Also ironically, the next financial report she would be working on was the one for FatLand National Bank, the bank that was funding the free subscriptions to GNT. She sat down in the office section of the retro Wright-type house, one of the most visible and most expensive in FatLand. She and Ed were both fairly short, which was why the Frank Lloyd Wright style didn't bother them. Taller people often objected to the ceilings.

Mira was taller, too. She wondered if Mira was unhappy partly because she didn't fit into this house. Or perhaps the house didn't fit her.

When she'd tried to hug her two days ago, the girl's bones had cut into her softness. "Ma, don't," Mira had said, gritting her teeth. "Please leave me alone."

Crushed, saddened, Joann had left Mira's room and its black lighting and neo-Goth posters. She had expected Mira also to follow that awful fashion of the 1990s in which many young people had pierced any and every part of their bodies, but Mira wasn't interested in piercing, as far as she knew.

As she started to dictate into the voice phone, Joann wondered if she should call Ed at work—in the field, no doubt, supervising testing today to make sure that certain more porous areas wouldn't encounter seepage in spring after the winter snows. But what could she possibly say that was new? On the other hand, Mira had shown some interest in the article in the newspaper, which was unusual for her. Was that reason enough to call her husband? She had those reports to complete, as well…

She decided not to call and turned to the assets section of the printout. Automatically she dictated the number into the voicephone. She then turned to the debit/expenditure section. *Now that was odd,* she thought.

According to the printout, FatLand National Bank's expenditures had gone down about 23 percent in one quarter. And that was just from one quarter to the next. If she traced it from the year before, they went down a whopping 34 percent. What was going on there?

She checked the numbers again, verified them with the printout, then put the sheet down. She clicked a key on the voicephone, which located, then dialed the number in response to her request to be connected with FatLand National Bank's statistics division.

"Hello," she said. "Is this Trudy? Joann Torelli here."

Chapter 5

Ava

THERE WERE TIMES when Ava had nightmares about being weighed in school in front of the entire class. With the nightmares also came shaming memories of the girls at camp in her bunk throwing around her underpants and running one pair up the flagpole, which would be announced later by the Assistant Director at morning assembly.

The best part of the nightmares, though, was waking up and knowing that they would not, could not happen now. As a matter of fact, on her good days, she thought of FatLand as what camp should have been—a place where one could appreciate nature and one's body and commune with both.

She had been assigned to cover a belly dancing performance tonight. And not just any performers—Leila's Best Belles were all fat. They toured FatLand three times a year. People went wild over them. It would be fun, she thought, to see what the fuss was about.

Ava put on one of her working outfits: a pair of black pants, black shirt, red print scarf, red shoes. She loved red shoes, but had not dared to wear them on the Other Side for fear that they would draw attention to her heft. *Oh, how trapped we were*, she thought, *and in how many ways*. She thought of Marcy again, but only momentarily, and resumed putting her digital camera inside her carryall.

She shut off the light and walked downstairs, where she put on the nightlight mainly to give herself a way to take out her keys. Many people in FatLand left their doors unlocked and did not even possess keys. If they really wanted a stat to crow about, she thought, why didn't the Board harp on our low crime rates as compared to the Other Side?

She herself feared at times that some powerful people on the Other Side would purposely send provocateurs into FatLand to try to foment fights and other recordable crime. But if they had done so, all their efforts had been in vain. Crime in FatLand, low from the beginning, was even lower now. Perhaps it also had something to do with FatLand's guaranteed social security/unemployment compensation for those out of work, however long they remained unemployed, and its free retraining and job-matching programs.

Or was it an economic issue at all? Difficult to say.

She walked the fourteen blocks to the FatLand Cultural Center. It was a fine sparkling cold night, with stars bright and hints of the Northern Lights flickering. Ava loved the Northern Lights almost as much as she loved FatLand. She watched as small breaths of red and green shimmered and curled, then vanished among blue trailers. Magnificent.

Once inside the center she saw several people she knew, including a few colleagues from other papers. They exchanged greetings, pleasantries, and a few jokes. Ava sat with her editor, Margaret, whom she knew would want to talk to her about the latest Board meeting. They would probably go for coffee and pastries afterward at the excellent and estimable Cherry Crossing coffee shop.

The lights dimmed. The music, suitably Middle Eastern in origin, began. Ava stared in surprise, then in pleasure as the attractive fat dancers made their way onto the stage. "Why didn't I see them before?" she whispered to Margaret. "They've been coming here for several years, haven't they?"

"At least four," Margaret answered. "Do you have your camera?"

"Sure do." Ava took it out of her carryall. "I think I'll—"

She stopped as a tall dancer made her way to the center of the stage. The golden light bathed her honey skin, making her belly shimmer with each shake and roll. Her long dark hair swirled as she dipped, then swung her body down, down, until her hair swept the floor. "Who is that?" Ava whispered, almost in awe.

Margaret consulted her program. "From what I can tell here, that is Amiyah. Says she's from Egypt."

"So she's really from there."

"According to this, yes."

Ava fell silent as Amiyah turned her back to the audience and began to shimmy, her legs liquid and golden again under her hip scarf.

Suddenly Ava began to feel something she hadn't felt in more than twenty years. At first she pushed it back in disgust. Then her body of its own accord started to feel hot in several places. She saw Amiyah smiling at the audience and sweating, a drop coursing down her honey colored belly. Then she caught Ava's eye and smiled.

Through the rest of the performance Ava had eyes for no one except Amiyah.

Chapter 6

Ava

DURING THE NEXT WEEK Ava found herself humming, something she hadn't done in more than twenty years. She found herself outside for no reason, looking at the stars. Leila's Best Belles were due back for another performance in another week. They had been sold out the first time.

It was not necessary for *FatLand Free News* reporters to interact regularly with their editors, for the most part. But she found Margaret talking to and mailing her more often than she had in all of the years she had been at the *News*. Did she know somehow that Ava was coming out of her shell? If that was what it was.

Ava found herself dressing with especial care the night of the second Best Belles performance. Instead of her usual black, she put on a light purple sparkly sweater bought, she admitted to herself with somewhat enjoyable guilt, for this occasion last week in Cammy's Cool Closet on Kate Richards O'Hare Boulevard (called O'Hare by FatLanders). The pants were a grey slinky material that harmonized with the light purple sweater. She felt magical, as if all the lights in the universe were reflecting from her. Her melon breasts and generous hips shimmered.

She turned and turned again in front of the mirror. *If she looks at me again and smiles, I'm going to go backstage,* she told herself. *If she doesn't...*

As she let herself out of the sleek townhouse and locked the door by reflex, Ava breathed in the clear frosty air and fastened her dark eyes on the austere beauty of the Pole Star.

Chapter 7

Dara

IF IT WASN'T *The FatLand Free News*, it was *The FatLand Courier Gazette* or *The FatLand Plain Writer.* Not by coincidence, the constitution of FatLand appeared in all three that first week of October.

WE THE PEOPLE OF FATLAND, in order to form a free and just State according to free and just principles, do ordain that the Territory of FatLand be open to those who accept that Fat People—people of heft, people of substance, people formerly styled "obese," people formerly derided as needing to lose weight or "overweight"—are entitled to the same rights as those once accorded freely to those deemed to be of average size or thin.

We hereby decree the following:

There shall be no mention of weight made in any office, establishment or facility, public or private, commercial or nonprofit, in FatLand. Any person who breaks this rule shall be fined the sum of one hundred thousand dollars on the first offense, one million dollars for the second offense, and banished from Fat-Land for the third offense. Nor shall any health personnel be allowed to use scales to weigh patients at any time. There shall be no scales in any schools of any level in FatLand, including private and public schools of the pre-school, kindergarten, elementary, middle, high school, community college, technical college, university/college levels.

There shall be no reference to level or division of weight or appearance in any establishment or facility or school or office in FatLand, public or private. There shall also be no reference to appearance of any kind, in any establishment or facility or school or office in FatLand, public or private.

There shall be no scales anywhere in FatLand, whether in establishments, facilities, schools, offices, or homes, public or private.

Any discrimination on the basis of weight, appearance, gender, sexual orientation, ethnicity, ethnic identification, religion, religious identification, or health in any establishment, office, facility, school, or hospital, public or private, shall lead to a suspension of license of business or practice until and unless it is proven beyond a strong doubt in a Grand Jury that such discrimination did not occur.

All the costs incurred by citizens of FatLand in health facilities by citizens of FatLand shall be completely covered by the Health Insurance Policy provided by The FatLand Mutual Assurance Associaton.

Health care outside facilities for citizens of FatLand as determined necessary by medical personnel shall also be completely covered by the Health Insurance Policy provided by The FatLand Mutual Assurance Association.

No FatLander shall be required at any time to eat any food s/he does not wish to eat. No FatLander shall be prohibited or stopped from eating any food s/he wishes to eat, providing that such food has been inspected and adjudged free of pernicious bacteria and/or contaminants by the FatLand Health Board or their lawful representative(s).

No FatLander shall be required at any time to engage in exercise that s/he does not wish to engage in.

A FatLander becomes a citizen upon residing in FatLand for two years if s/he has not broken any of the laws of FatLand and has not transgressed against the Constitution of FatLand in letter or in spirit.

No FatLander shall be made to travel to other states/countries/national entities if s/he does not wish to do so.

A FatLander wishing to be a member of the Board shall have resided in FatLand for at least five years, shall have gained citizenship, and shall have evinced a clear and abiding interest in and concern for the welfare and happiness of FatLand and FatLanders. S/he shall be at least 25 years of age.

WELL, THERE IT WAS, in clear print on the terminal screen and in black and white print in all the newspapers, Dara Goldenberg thought as she sipped her morning mocha and munched a blueberry bagel with strawberry cream cheese (she liked lox on plain bagels, but not in the morning). That GymNotTrim affair was starting to take on a life of its own, as Alvin had warned in their last meeting. Reevie, his wife and her good friend, was already putting together a skit about it to be sent to all the elementary schools in FatLand. The Board was due to meet again in two weeks.

"They can't get away with this!" Alvin had fumed when they'd met. "The Constitution says clearly that people shall not be made to exercise if they don't wish to!"

She'd agreed completely with him on principle. Her parents had come to FatLand seeking a haven from dieting and exercise and look-sist coercion. As a FatLander she had grown up eating what she wished, moving as she wished, and thinking what she wished.

The problem was that now, as one of the two medical members of the FatLand Board, she found that her life had become extremely complicated by the Health Assurance Company's pronouncement and offer.

Dara was short, dark-haired and softly curvy. She had been sought after as a girlfriend and date since her early days in kindergarten. Now at twenty-nine she was having an affair with Sandor Forman, the Chair of the Board and founder of GymNotTrim.

At first she had figured he was attracted to her for the usual reasons—her figure, her softness, her smile. Now she was having second and third thoughts, especially after their last session in her light blue sky-and-ocean-themed bedroom.

"Darry," Sandor had whispered as they lay in the afterglow of superb coming together, "I have to ask you something."

Marriage? She shuddered, although delightfully. She wasn't ready.

"How do you as a physician feel about the latest figures on FatLand mortality?"

Oh. So that was what he was driving at. "I feel just fine about it. Why?"

"You don't think there's anything a little—strange about those figures?"

"Not at all. We compared them with the most recent readings and had them checked over by two different companies. We are quite confident in them."

He sighed. "So I take it you wouldn't be willing to state that you felt there might be a question about those figures and that FatLanders would benefit from the GymNotTrim offer?"

"I take it that you would like me to make such a statement?"

He sighed again. "I'm in sort of a pickle—damned if I do, and damned if I don't. If I don't make any comment, certain people on the Other Side and in GymNotTrim will wonder why I'm not trying to boost their sales. If I do make a comment, FatLanders will wonder why. They're already wondering why, as a matter of fact."

"Let me get this straight, then," Dara said, shifting slightly away from him. "You want me to talk with Alvin and tell him that I believe the mortality figures are not correct? He'll never buy that. He would probably respect a disagreement about the GymNotTrim offer if it seemed honest to him."

Sandor sighed and reached for her. "Sugar, don't go away from me," he whispered.

She sighed and didn't return the pressure on his hand, but didn't let go of it, either.

Chapter 8

Alvin

ALVIN GAZED INTO REEVIE'S EYES, then looked meaningfully up and down her body. He loved playing with Reevie's breasts, Reevie's stomach—all of her, actually. But most of all, he loved being inside Reevie. Sometimes he never wanted to come out. He had told her as much a few times. Each time she answered, "Then don't come out. Just stay inside me."

What luck or accident or fate or karma caused two human beings to come together and not just love each other, but fit together as they did, inside and out? Some people, he knew, would say that he and Reevie had been lovers in another life, or that they had both done very good things in previous lives, and that for this, they reaped the reward.

He burrowed down into her, licking her stomach, sniffing her pubis, which always made her laugh because his mustache tickled. He enfolded the soft flesh of her midriff in his hands, then let it go, and ran his hands over her stomach and lush upper thighs, causing her to sigh. He teased her soft upper arms and ran his fingers under them, causing her to giggle.

"Alvin," she whispered.

He dug his fingers gently into her vulva and tenderly pushed down into her again, teasing, then pushing her clitoris as he did so. She moaned. It excited him no end when she moaned and cried. He got harder and pushed further into her again. She rose up to meet him. They wrestled in harmony as they turned in the strong bed and she was now on top of him, pushing down in him, taking all of him in, setting the pace.

She ran her fingers over his thick strongly muscled arms and teased his capable brown fingers one by one, taking the middle one in her mouth. "Tease," he said under his breath, grinning.

"That's right," she agreed. She continued to lick his third finger until he was even harder in her and they pushed into each other, turning again so that both were sitting and facing each other. She loved this. He and she were now equal and together and all of her torso rubbed against his. She thrilled to the touch of his stomach flesh and those muscles against her breasts and stomach. She kissed him strongly and bit his lip.

"Hey," he yelled, and lunged for her, biting her nipple. She yelled in turn and grabbed his face, kissing his eyes, mouth, nose, chin, and the delicate flesh of his neck.

They spiralled down again onto the bed, grasping each other and moving deeper into wonder.

WHEN THE PHONE RANG an hour later, they were both sleeping so soundly that it took two sets of rings to rouse them. Alvin answered sleepily, mechanically. "'Lo?"

"Alvin," a familiar voice said on the other end, "this is Dara. I need to see you as soon as possible."

Chapter 9

Mira

SHE STOOD NEXT TO THE STEEL GATE and barracks-type building that comprised the border crossing from FatLand to the Other Side.

A copy of the FatLand Constitution was posted on the side of the barracks. Since there was no line for the crossing or checkpoint, she did not have time to look at it. Just as well, she thought. The Constitution was a joke, anyway.

No discrimination on the basis of weight. But had she ever experienced anything else? The visits by social workers, humiliating her mom and dad, but herself most of all. The looks and giggles in her classes. The fingerpointing at social events—when she had gone to them, early in high school, before she had learned not to. The difficulty of getting clothes that fit, and being something of a laughingstock when she had to parade around in gym class in a uniform three sizes too big (and that was euphemistic, since FatLand uniforms started at a size she had never been in her entire life).

Goodbye to what, she thought. *I'm sorry about this, mom and dad and Jess, but this country never gave me a thing. I am a complete fish out of water here. I would like to know what it's like to date, not to be laughed at, not to have people pointing at me, pitying me.*

Before she handed her papers to the official at the checkpoint, she experienced a searing realization that her parents had gone through all of what she had, but on the Other Side.

"We are required to ask you this by law," the official intoned. "Has any person or agency coerced you to leave FatLand?"

"No."

"Did you experience any problems in FatLand which are leading you to seek exit from FatLand?"

"Oh, for goodness sake, look at me!" she said, exasperated. "My problem is plain as day. I am thin in a fat country!"

"Ms. Torelli," the official said in a kind voice, "we are really only referring to medical and financial problems here."

"No!"

"Do you realize that once you leave FatLand, you may not be able to secure entrance again without a Re-entrance Visa, which may take up to six months to obtain?"

"Yes." She was sad at the thought of not seeing her parents again for months, and Jess, but she was so tired of sitting in her room and not seeing people, not moving, trying to fit in when fitting in was impossible.

"Please sign the bottom of this paper indicating that you have been asked and have answered these questions."

She sighed.

"I am empowered to ask you if you have the prospect of employment on the Other Side, Ms. Torelli."

"I do."

The official nodded. "Good luck, then."

"Thanks."

He opened the door and led her to the checkpoint. "I'm sorry," he said.

"I was," she said. "But not anymore."

Mira walked the fifty yards to the entrance house at the Other Side. *Welcome to the United States of America,* she read. *Flagstone Crossing and Checkpoint.*

"Hi," she said to the official on the Other Side. "Here are my papers."

He looked at her. "Well, hello," he grinned. "Nice to see you here. Would you like to have a seat while we check your papers? Coffee's over there, and tea and hot chocolate. I made the hot chocolate a few minutes ago, so it's fresh. We're not really supposed to offer it because of the Pro-Health Laws, but I say that we can at least be hospitable to people who make the effort to come over. "

Mira looked back at him, savoring, delighting in the official's openly appreciative look. "Sounds good to me," she said, smiling for the first time in years. "I love hot chocolate."

Chapter 10

Reevie

As she drove along the streets leading to the border, Reevie thought of the meeting she and Alvin had had with Dara. She knew something was up when Dara had asked them to meet not at one of their houses, which they had done for months, but in an out-of-the-way restaurant frequented by a late-night crowd.

"Angling for a change of scene?" she had greeted her friend.

To her surprise, Dara had not grinned in return. Instead she said rather hesitantly and stiffly, "Sorry to get you out so late."

"Dara," Reevie said as Alvin walked in, "whatever is the matter?"

"Well—" Dara had looked extremely embarrassed and had stared at the floor. "I was having some second thoughts about those mortality statistics."

Now it was Alvin's turn to look surprised. "Why?"

"Well, there were certain parts of the latest study methodology that sounded to me like shortcuts."

"Why didn't you say something about this before?" Alvin asked.

"I only realized it today, when I had time to think about it more."

"What do you think should be done?"

"I think we should call in another research group."

"Another one? After all this? We've had two already."

"That's why we need a third."

"Do you really think they'll find anything that different?"

"No, but we have to make sure."

Alvin looked at her. "Dara," he said, "you think this is important enough to waste more of FatLand's resources?" He'd put it that baldly, that pointblank. Alvin didn't get annoyed often.

"Yes. With something like this, we have to be absolutely certain. There can be no questions."

"With mortality studies there will always be questions," Alvin said. "But if you're so concerned about it, I suppose we can find another agency."

"I already have one in mind."

Chapter 11

Reevie

THAT WAS QUICK, Reevie thought as she drove up to the border checkpoint. Dara had gotten the name of the agency even before getting Alvin's okay. After the strangely awkward meeting had ended she'd said to Alvin, "Something's going on here."

"She seemed nervous," he said. "And worried. That's not like Dara. Usually she's the most even-tempered person in the world."

"No, you're usually the most even-tempered person in the world," Reevie'd said. But she knew he wouldn't be even-tempered at all if he knew what she was doing now and where she was going.

Every two months or so Reevie met with a group called FatAnd-Proud on the Other Side. They were a group of fat activists who didn't believe in living in a "segregated society," as they styled FatLand. They believed in trying to reform the Other Side so fat people could live there in peace amd harmony.

"But you're the majority there," Reevie had pointed out to them at their first meeting with her on the Other Side after she had moved to FatLand so many years ago. "And yet you still can't get out from under the yoke of the diet specialists and experts. After all this time. Study after study shows that dieting doesn't work, that fat people live as long as or longer than thin people when they get the same health coverage and good care and no harangues about their weight. Yet the Diet Empire keeps its stranglehold on your society. And you still think this is going to change, after all of your efforts have been in vain?"

"It will change," one of them had prophesied. "You're leaving and giving up just when things are starting to happen."

Things had indeed started to happen, Reevie remembered. Fat kids taken from their parents on the pretext of "abuse." A fat Ms. America candidate spit on by one of the other candidates. Taxes on anything with sugar in it.

And yet, Reevie thought, things had been different for a little while, although maybe because of FatLand itself. More fat women and men had started to be on TV on the Other Side. At one point fat kids were no longer picked on as much, partly because of sensitivity training for teachers and principals and guidance counselors. More fat-accepting doctors had graduated from medical schools, and doctors in general were no longer pushing their fat patients to try to lose weight.

But then—

Reevie reached the checkpoint and handed her papers to the official, who knew her and Alvin. "Get back soon," the official said. "We'll send someone to rescue you if they try anything."

Reevie laughed each time she heard this. "You wouldn't have to send anyone. I'd threaten to take people with me back to FatLand and they'd let me go like *this*." She snapped her fingers.

Of course Alvin would be worried and angry if he knew what she was doing and where she was going. He was dead set against any meetings with fat acceptance activists on the Other Side.

"They have nothing there," he said when she'd mentioned the activists. "And yet they persist. I consider that both shortsighted and dangerous. Promise me you would never do such a thing."

She'd promised.

And lied.

The one lie of her marriage, and she kept hoping with each visit that nothing would happen to reveal her forays into the Other Side. Goodness knows she didn't look forward to them, didn't look forward to the suspicious sullen glances of the official on the Other Side's checkpoint, or to the stares of the thin people left on the Other Side when she pulled into their meeting place, a restaurant in many ways similar to the one where she and Alvin and Dara had held their rather strange-feeling meeting.

But someone had to meet with them, she thought. Occasionally she entertained ideas of trying to convert one or two of the activists to living in FatLand, but she dropped them when they started to talk. These

FAAs were committed to making the Other Side more fat-accepting, and many of them had been in the movement for over 20 years, as long as she and Alvin had been in FatLand. She had to admire that kind of determination.

Chapter 12

Ava

"I CAN'T BELIEVE IT," Ava whispered as Amiyah ushered her into the rather skimpy hotel room she occupied when she performed in FatLand. "If I'd known, I'd have invited you to stay with me."

"You could not know," Amiyah said, smiling. With the permission of the leader of Leila's Best Belles, Ava had asked Amiyah if she would consent to be interviewed. Both Leila, the leader, and Amiyah had thought it an excellent idea, as had Margaret, her editor. "Slice of life stuff on a fat beautiful woman," Margaret had said approvingly. "Can't get enough of that."

"So is this where the troupe stays when you all come to town?" Ava asked, taking out her Pod3 and clicking it to record the interview.

"Usually," Amiyah said, lying down on the double bed and stretching out. Ava's heart skipped a beat.

"I know you have a lot of fans here," she said, trying to stay focused. "What is special for you about performing in FatLand?"

"We feel we are among our own," Amiyah said.

"Was it difficult for you," Ava asked, "as a fat woman growing up in Egypt?"

"Not most of the time," Amiyah said. "There are still a lot of men who appreciate fat beautiful women there." She beamed. "Like you."

Ava's face grew hot, as it hadn't since her first months with Marcy. "Thanks, but—" She stopped as Amiyah started to take off her top piece. She stared in confused and growing excitement as Amiyah stood up.

"How did you know?" she whispered, her eyes trying not to travel to Amiyah's large light olive-tan breasts with their hard brown nipples, but failing. She had trouble breathing as Amiyah now stood over her and put Ava's right hand on one of them.

"I didn't know," Amiyah said, smiling as Ava leaned into the nipple with her mouth and started to lick it. "I just hoped."

Chapter 13

Ed

ED STOOD AND LOOKED AT THE HOUSE he and Joann and Jesse and Mira had occupied for twenty-one years. *A lot of love in this house,* he thought. *And sadness.* He thought of the note he and Joann had received from Mira a few days before.

Dear Mom and Dad,

I knew you'd be worried about me, so I am writing this note. I am living on the Other Side now, in Jeffreys. It is about five hundred miles from the border. I have just been hired as a Gym-NotTrim trainer, which was what I had hoped for. They really like me and they say I will probably move up to Trainer Supervisor in a matter of months.

Mom and Dad and Jesse, I don't think you knew or even imagined what it was like for me, living in FatLand. I felt as if every fiber of my being was just wrong there. I could never gain weight. I could never even think of myself as having a fat person in me waiting to come out. I feel thin and spare and that is what I am. People here appreciate that, even some of the fat people.

And I am dating now. I have two men who call me a lot, and I could have more, but I want to start slowly, at first.

Please don't worry about me. I am so much happier here than I could have imagined possible. I will write to you as often as I can. Maybe one day we can meet. Please be happy and happy for me.

Much Love,
Your Daughter Mira

Ed ran through the note in his mind. How ironic that Mira had voiced the same thoughts, in reverse, that had driven him and Joann to find a home in FatLand.

Growing up, he had always been fat. And yet somehow he had never felt wrong as a fat person. So many people had pushed him to try to lose weight, including his parents, his brother, his dates. It had been impossible to explain to them that he felt fine the way he was. He certainly cycled and walked enough, even jogged during his one try at dieting. His burly body had some muscles on it, although he didn't work out much, preferring to give most of his energy to his job as soil tester, which he loved. Joann, he knew, had had much the same experience—feeling fine in her lovely fat body, not quite understanding why everyone wanted to make her thinner.

Except for him, of course. Unlike some of his friends, fat and thin, he had always liked heavier women. He loved the way their bodies swam and jiggled in their clothes. He loved hugging them. His mom, who was always trying to lose weight, was a fat woman herself. Except for his wife, he thought she was the most beautiful woman in the world, and wished she had stopped trying. That way maybe she wouldn't have dieted herself into ill health. And for what? For twenty pounds, which was the most she'd ever lost and which she kept regaining?

He thought of one of the signs in a coffee shop he and Joann used to go to. "DIETING = DIEING MINUS THE 'T'."

They were right in regards to his mother. Her heart had been severely affected by constant dieting, yo-yoing, gaining, losing, regaining. He remembered the call on a cold winter's day, and the rush to the hospital on the Other Side only to find out that she'd gone before he could talk to her after twenty years. And holding her hand while a nurse had the nerve to comment to him, a FatLander, that his mother might have lived longer if she'd lost some weight!

Ever since then Ed had avoided all thoughts of the Other Side. He wondered if Mira expected them to come to visit her there; hoped not. But if Joann wanted them to go—

I miss her, though, he thought as he looked at the house in the quickly setting winter sun.

He didn't expect the reporter who confronted him at the edge of the back patio and said, "Mr. Torelli, I wonder if you'd like to comment on your daughter's new job with GymNotTrim on the Other Side."

"Why should I comment?" he said. "If she's happy, then I'm happy for her."

The reporter said, "But as the spokesperson for their 'You don't want to live in FatLand' campaign?"

"What?" he said, incredulous.

"You didn't know?"

"No!"

"Let me show you the video."

Sick at heart, Ed watched as the reporter clicked his Pod3 and played the video. It showed a thin but glowing Mira wearing a shiny yellow bikini and saying in a caressing voice, "If you come here," with a picture of GymNotTrim in the background, "you won't have to go *there.*" And the scene shifted quickly to a picture of three smiling fat people with the "Welcome to FatLand" sign in the background.

"Have a lot of people seen this?" he asked the reporter.

"Not yet."

"Well, they're going to," he said, walking toward the back door as the reporter followed. "And thanks for the tip."

Chapter 14

Reevie

HEART BEATING FASTER, eyes glued to the door of The Laurels Diner, Reevie waited for the members of FatAndProud to come.

Why am I always here first? she wondered. *I even hate the way the owner looks at me, although this is where everyone comes to get real food on the Other Side. In Colorado, anyway. How can they stand it?*

Each time she was here she realized she had forgotten what it was like to have to develop a "thick skin" so that people's stares and comments didn't bother her. That alone made it worth living in Fatland. One didn't have to wear a "thick skin."

But those here, on the Other Side, lived the lives of proud outcasts—those not marching in step with the mainstream, those building their own paths and dancing on the edges. In a way it was a proud life, striking out from the crowd, daring to live against the wind, against convention—but even more, to risk the hell of an Other Side Pro-Health Prison. Reevie shuddered, trying not to think of the stories she had heard.

They had rather lost that in FatLand. One simply didn't have to live counter there, as a fat person. She'd found out in FatLand what it was like to be able to feel part of the mainstream, part of the setters of convention. Did most people in FatLand feel as if they were part of the mainstream now? She had never thought to ask anyone. She admitted to herself with some embarrassment that it felt damned fine to be able to live as part of the mainstream.

Here, on the Other Side, there were millions of fat people who would be perfectly happy to live the most staid of conventional lives, but they were not allowed to do so simply because of their body shapes and sizes. It was bizarre, when you got down to it.

IRENA WAS THE FIRST ONE to arrive. She spied Reevie at the table toward the back of the diner and nodded. Sitting down, she took out her glasses and looked at the menu, then at Reevie. "Waited for us to order?" she said, making it a question even though she knew the answer.

"Might as well," Reevie said. "Consider it my treat." She always said that, in one form or another.

Shermaine arrived next. She waved. "How's it going, girlfriend?" she greeted Reevie from the front of the restaurant.

Reevie smiled and said, "It's good," although all of it wasn't.

Sitting down next to Reevie, Shermaine said, "You look a little worried."

"Some strange things are occurring."

"Like that GymNotTrim thing?"

"What GymNotTrim thing?"

"Oh lord," Shermaine said. "You didn't see it yet?"

"I only know that they're offering free subscriptions to FatLanders who want to join."

"They're offering something very different here," Shermaine said.

"Like?"

"I brought the smartdisk," Irena said, and put it on the pod. "Let's wait until the others get here."

The "others" that evening turned out to be Barbara and Valerie. They all greeted each other and ordered, having agreed to play the disk for Reevie after dinner when Barbara noted she might not want to eat if she saw it before.

"Try the meatloaf with mushroom gravy," Irena said. "They do it really well here."

But Reevie was an Italian food junkie and ordered the *spaghetti alla rosa* instead, with a serving of calamari on the side. And a glass of the house white, which was not at all bad for a diner, she noted as she toasted the meeting: "To fat pride."

"To fat pride," they chorused as Irena sipped her *cafe au lait,* Shermaine touched her lips to a Bloody Mary, Barbara inhaled her herbal tea, and Valerie imbibed a Johnny Walker Black Label on the rocks.

Most of these foods and beverages were forbidden, of course, or came with a stiff Non-Approved Food Tax, And "fat" people weren't supposed to be consuming them anyway. But The Laurels made up for its sundry lawbreaking by charging rather high prices. However, as they assured each other each time, it was worth it.

Reevie watched the waiter all through the taking of the orders and serving of the food, but saw nothing disrespectful or threatening in his behavior. She told this to Shermaine, who laughed and said, "They get a lot of business from your side these days."

"What?"

"You don't know?" Irena said as she carefully cut into her chicken *a l'orange.*

"Know what?"

"Seems it's the thing for teenagers from your side to do these days."

"Come here for a meal, you mean?"

"That. And to see some thinner people."

Reevie sighed. "Why is it that teenagers seem to know exactly how to press our buttons?"

Valerie laughed. "Don't worry about it. They always have, and they always will. So far there's been no report of any misbehavior from your young ones. Be glad for that."

Reevie said, "In a way I almost wish they would misbehave. But I suppose it's best not."

Irena, who wore a bright red sweater that brought out her magnificent sloping shoulders and long pear breasts, said, "They won't misbehave too much if they're happy."

"See?" Reevie said. "But you don't want to be there and stay happy."

"Nope," Barbara said. She was carefully attired in a navy wool poncho and matching pants. "We prefer to push the envelope here and shake the tree."

"So how is shaking the tree going?" Reevie asked after they'd ordered dessert (still no sign of disrespect from the waiter, who turned out to be Italian by nationality. Reevie figured that might make a difference). "Do you see any chance to at least soften the Pro-Health

Laws?"

"Fourteen states have resolutions to amend," Irena said. "But there may be another suit right here in Colorado, of all places."

"What kind of suit?" Reevie asked.

"There's a rumor," Shermaine said, "that it will concern someone from FatLand."

"Who?"

"It may be connected with this," Barbara said, and punched the Pod3 button.

The advertisement began to roll. Mira's luminous eyes danced as she recited the lines of the script.

"So," Reevie said almost in a whisper. "One hand praises us, the other hand damns us."

"Free subscriptions for you," Valerie said, "and more business for us because we're supposed to be deathly afraid of turning into you."

"You afraid?" Shermaine said.

"The only deaths that will occur," Barbara said, "are when people here get their bills from GymNotTrim. Or go to an AG prison."

Reevie shivered.

Valerie said, "It's that they sort of sentence you to a life there. You can only get out if you're going to die or your doctor writes them a note."

"Great," Reevie said. "I hope they don't think they're going to pull that in FatLand."

"Girlfriend, you better make damned sure they don't," Shermaine said.

All through dessert—a piece of infamous and enchanting chocolate almond mud cake with fresh whipped cream—Reevie kept remembering the advertisement. She also planned what she would say if Alvin decided to call the friend's house she was supposed to be visiting and the friend forgot her coached lines.

The one lie, she thought again. *But it's worth it.*

Chapter 15

Sandor

"WHAT DO YOU SEE WHEN YOU SEE YOURSELF in the mirror every morning?"

That was the question his fat acceptance activist parents had asked him every morning. And every morning he had answered them, "I see a strong healthy mind in a strong healthy body." It was what they wanted to hear, and there was no reason for him not to say it or feel that he was lying about it. He felt strong and healthy and happy, most of the time.

Then suddenly, at the age of 18, his freshman year in college, he had lost forty pounds.

He didn't know why, had no idea as to what caused the weight loss. None of his professors at FatLand University had said anything. But there had been a lot of raised eyebrows in the dorm halls and a lot of whispers.

He thought from time to time that maybe he had not been eating as much as he had at home, but he knew quite well by now that eating just a little less wouldn't account for his losing forty pounds.

Since he was the shy type, he hadn't been talking much to girls before the weight loss. He became even shyer after. He mostly stayed in his room and read, skipped a few more classes than he had previously. In his reading he discovered Charles Atlas. And he realized that there were no gyms in FatLand.

This of course was partly because of the part of the constitution that decreed that no FatLander should be subject to mandatory exercise. But as he read, he found out that people could change the shapes of their bodies by exercising. What he had lost, he could gain back in muscle.

He started with two sets of dumbbells and worked his way up. Exercise programs were neither discouraged nor encouraged at FatLand University. They simply didn't exist.

Within six weeks he had men in the dorm asking if he could teach them how to build muscles. Within eight weeks he had women in the dorm asking if he could teach them how to build both muscles and curves.

GymNotTrim opened the following year, as mostly his brainchild, with the help of two other men in the dorm and a dean who was impressed by Sandor's perseverance and business sense.

"Lose the tiredness, not the weight!" the first ad for GymNotTrim read. "Gain energy and have fun!" the second ad read.

He pioneered some wild and totally off-the-wall features at Gym-NotTrim, such as the carousel you had to bicycle on, the Ferris wheel with arm muscle building equipment, the Super Juice Bar, which featured juices, other beverages, bread, bagels, pastries, newspapers, computer terminals, and plenty of places to chat, and the most controversial item of all, but a gigantic hit—the clothing-optional pool that was open 24 hours a day.

Never had exercising been so much fun.

For the first five years after its opening, FatLanders flocked to Gym-NotTrim. GymNotTrim garnered almost weekly attention from the three official FatLand newspapers, which praised it—and him—constantly for innovative and non-weight-based techniques. Sandor felt as if he were treading on air.

Then attendance increased more slowly. By its seventh year Gym-NotTrim saw its numbers down two percent.

Its board met and recommended changes. The numbers went down even further.

"I think you've simply reached the saturation point," a sensible board member said. "Your management is fine. As long as you keep most of the people you have—"

"But FatLand's population is increasing," Sandor pointed out. "And yet our attendance is off."

"Diversify, man," the member said. "T-shirts, clothes, equipment, even parties and dances. Sponsor picnic evenings. Go social."

Sandor thanked the member and went to work. GymNotTrim's attendance zoomed upwards again. The board and he were happy campers, literally—GymNotTrim sponsored its own summer camp, but for adults, complete with bunks and counselors and all. It was a smash.

Then a year ago came the offer from CompleteFitness on the Other Side. In return for buying out GymNotTrim, Sandor and the other board members would receive $20 million in preferred options and rather large dividends.

"That would be fine," Sandor said, "provided you maintain our operating policy and message. No weight loss. Only exercise and fun."

"I don't think we can do that," the CompleteFitness CEO said.

"Too bad, then," Sandor said. "You're losing a great add-on."

"And you're losing the chance to break into the USA, which is what you've always wanted."

Sandor cursed silently. How had the CEO known? "But if we break into the USA with a weight loss theme, I'll get run out of FatLand."

"Why should FatLanders care about what others here think? They never did before."

"That's because they feel no one there really cares about what they think," Sandor said.

"Tell you what," the CEO said. "I think it'll work if you start off with a slight weight loss message, then revamp it. That will be more in line with your FatLand policy, and no one will be the wiser. You've got some great ideas that I think will catch on here in a big way. And my offer still stands."

"I would want to maintain control of the FatLand franchises, though."

"Agreed."

And that, Sandor thought, was what happened when you sold your soul to the devil for more markets.

His stomach turned sour when he thought of the disk he had just seen. The worst part, of course, was that the leadership of CompleteFitness had not even seen fit to alert him to the advertisement. He had had to receive it anonymously, from a group on the Other Side called FatAndProud.

Pushing away his morning coffee and English muffin with butter and strawberry jam, Sandor dialed a number on the smartphone. "I want to speak to Winston Stark," he said. "Now."

Chapter 16

Amiyah

THE WOMAN WHO CALLED HERSELF AMIYAH looked at herself in the mirror and smiled. As long as she could remember she had been told that she was beautiful. And as long as she could remember, she had been heavy or fat. Why, she wondered, was it a problem for Americans to admit that someone could be both pretty and fat? When she danced for them, they seemed to have no trouble admitting both.

She thought of Ava, whom she felt was also beautiful and fat. It was such a shame that such a beautiful woman had to go through life not being able to claim her beauty. The fat people in the USA had to make FatLand for themselves. America was supposed to be so much better than Egypt, but in this it fell short. What good was it to say you were a democracy with equal rights for all when you ignored and even hated half your citizens?

Her fingers traced the curves and hills of Ava's body in thought. She remembered with delight the softness of Ava's melon breasts and her sloping hips and yielding thighs and her generous and plush behind.

On the other hand, in Egypt it was forbidden for a woman to love other women. But more and more women were discovering the delights of loving women, although they could not admit their love. Amiyah had loved both women and men. She did not see why it should be forbidden to love anyone. *Our bodies come from God. Why not use them to give us pleasure if we do not hurt anyone and instead give much pleasure too?*

Before Ava, there had been a man in the USA she had loved. He still sent her letters and flowers and jewels. She wore some of the jewels at times when she performed.

She was just about to dress for her next performance when the phone rang.

"Amiyah," a voice said, "my name is Sandor Forman and I am the CEO of GymNotTrim."

Chapter 17

Joann

THE REPORTERS HAD BEEN CAMPED OUTSIDE the Torelli house for four days. Each day Joann opened the door and shut it in their faces, but left hot rolls with butter and bagels with cream cheese and cups of coffee. The reporters, especially those from the USA/Other Side, where such foods were essentially forbidden, agreed that it was by far the nicest "stakeout" they had ever been on.

Joann stared at the wooden door that shut out part of the front driveway. She knew she couldn't blame the reporters for needing to do their jobs. And yet there was something so embarrassingly shameful about being the parents of the first person from FatLand to emigrate to the USA that she could not think of talking to reporters.

The reporters also hounded Ed when he came back each evening after work. He brushed them off with a curt "No comment" and barreled in through the front door, his burly strength maintaining order by veiled threat. He assumed that none of the reporters wanted to get kicked out headfirst.

"We thought we could somehow construct the perfect society," Joann said to him in the study that night. They were both sipping brandies in an effort to calm themselves. "A place no one would want to leave. Even thin people."

"When you're different," Ed said, shrugging his meaty, strong freckled shoulders, "there are always people who will make you feel different, whether or not they mean to."

"Do you think she's happier now?"

"She sounded happier."

"Are Jesse's friends giving him a hard time about this?"

"Not yet."

"Are we going to talk to the reporters eventually?"

"I don't know."

"Do you think we should leave FatLand?"

"Absolutely not!"

"Are we going to give the radio a quote? We always liked radio better." Joann drew her hand wearily across her eyes. And yet all the time she was looking into the rainbow deep in her brandy glass, she was wondering if the reporters would be interested in a completely different story.

Chapter 18

Margaret

THERE ARE NO COINCIDENCES. Only reasons.

She was amused and pleased to see that between the self-awakening and renaissance occasioned by a knee-weakening affair, Ava had found time to do some damningly accurate research and send a report.

She was not so pleased to see what was written in it, although it was something part of her had known all along. As she read Ava's report, she sighed. Sins coming home to roost? More like rejection, in this case.

"Stark's goal," Ava had keyed, "seems to be to buy out GymNotTrim, sack Forman, and move his own people into control. Forman seemed to be hot for the deal, but didn't sign. Wonder if he's having second thoughts. That would be a first, for him."

What Ava didn't know—or at least, Margaret didn't think she knew—was that Stark had asked her, Margaret, several times to be his mistress.

It was one of those juicy ironies that smacked of hypocrisy and ambivalence. Here was Stark, on the one hand, promoting with all fervor and might Complete Fitness, a weight-loss corporate body that pretended to be concerned about people's fitness. Stark's latest wife, a svelte young Russian woman Stark had met through an agency promising Russian brides who were eager to please, was one of the models for Complete Fitness. In its advertisement, Lyudmila said—amid a flurry of situps, jumping jacks, rowing exercises, and weightlifting—that she went there every day.

And yet not a week passed without a phone call (how he kept finding her unlisted FatLand numbers, Margaret did not like to think, although she had an idea), a bouquet, a note, even an email from Stark.

She and Stark had met in college. She remembered her pre-Fat-Land days vaguely, or would have, if Stark did not keep bringing them back into focus by his unseen but insistent presence. Margaret Clancy was a tall, buxom, red-haired girl with cat-green eyes, a dry wit, and a tendency to dance on the rooftop of the science building in the rain. Perhaps it was the dance, more than anything else, that Stark had fallen in love with—or said that he had.

He brought her silly but endearing poems on the tops of matchbooks from different restaurants, red melted-wax candles with one rose on top, funny scarves and rings from little places in Back Bay before it became super-fashionable. She sort of knew he was after some kind of mogulship in corporatehood, even then, but she didn't care much. That didn't concern the here and now. Margaret continued to dance on the roof of the science building.

Then he went to law school and Margaret went to journalism school. They continued to correspond and see each other. He didn't get to Columbia every week, but she knew he had a supremely hectic schedule and didn't press.

Finally they both graduated. He informed her that he had passed the bar exam, and that he was coming for a very important talk.

Heart beating and sending waves of pink into her cheeks, Margaret put on her best green dress, the one that made her boobs into round apples and her eyes into emeralds. When the knock sounded, she opened the door.

"Hello, Margaret."

"Hello, Win."

"Margaret, I'd like you to meet someone. This is Anne."

From the first dutiful handshake and obligatory smile—Anne was about 5 foot 3 and wore a blue suit that ran over her bones in places where curves on other women might have padded—Margaret's disappointment and anger pulsed into her eyes in waves, even as she said, "Nice to meet you, Anne. Hope you'll have a great time here."

Later, as Anne went (perhaps purposely) to powder her nose, Margaret's eyes turned bright with unshed tears as she said quietly, "Why?"

"She's very necessary to me," Winston explained. "Her father has an interest in a place called Complete Fitness. It's going to take off big. I can get in on the ground floor."

"Glad it's so clear," Margaret said. "Does Anne know this charming fact?"

"Of course not," Winston said. "What do you take me for?"

I took you for mine, Margaret thought but did not say.

Resigned to wiping Winston out of her life, Margaret had come to FatLand two months later. She had worked for two FatLand newspapers and had started her own three years after that.

Then, half a year after the creation of her newspaper—with her assets, such as they were, on very shaky financial ground—Winston had sent her a note. "Margaret, I miss you so much. Can we meet again, just once, for old time's sake, if you don't want to see me after?"

She'd consented reluctantly, mostly because she had wanted, had hoped, had needed somehow to hear from Winston that things were not going at all well with Anne, that he'd made a mistake, that he wanted Margaret in his life.

Instead—

"The FatLand Free News has a good reputation even here," Winston had greeted her. "Too bad it's a bit shaky capital-wise."

"Why do you care?" she fired back.

"I care because I care about you," he said. "Now let me invest and be a silent partner. It's the least I can do."

She'd let him, mostly because she wasn't sure how long *The FatLand Free News* could survive without a much-needed injection of funds.

But then—

"Margaret, I've taken a room at the FatLand Premiere Fois. Say you'll come."

"Winston—"

"Don't worry, I won't make you at all uncomfortable. We'll have a drink. Drink to our partnership. That's all."

But Winston had drunk a few times—then a few too many—to their partnership. And then—

"Winston, I can't. You're married, besides everything else."

"And you're juicy and delicious."

"Then why didn't you marry me?"

"Thin is right for parties. Fat is right in bed."

She'd raised herself to stare at him. "And you are right out of here, mister."

Of course she had been the one who'd left. Holding her long skirt in her hand so she wouldn't trip down the curved stairway, she'd sailed out, holding her head high.

A week later, when she could trust herself to speak and write to him, she'd written, "As far as I am concerned, our previous agreement re *The FatLand Free News* is negated."

He'd written back, "It is not negated. I stand by it, now and forever."

Guilty at taking his money, but relieved to know that she wouldn't have to cut back drastically on staff or quality, Margaret had tried to rationalize all these years that he owed her this. As a silent partner, he had never interfered in the running of the paper. And she had found ways to evade most of his notes and calls, answering emails every so often with single curt sentences.

But now—

It does not surprise me in the least, she keyed to Ava. *Good work. Keep it coming.*

However, it won't stop there, she thought. He wants more than just GymNotTrim.

A line from a folk song, the kind she'd liked to sing sitting on the grass in front of the dorm lounge, wafted back to her. "All your cities I will burn…"

He's the one who married, she thought. *I didn't. Why does he think he can have exactly what he wants when he wants it?*

Why does anyone think he can have anything, another part of her mind answered. *He thinks he deserves it.*

Chapter 19

Winston

WINSTON LOOKED DOWN to where the sign indicated the FatLand border and checkpoint. She was there. Someplace. Moving around her office, typing something, mapping out a story or a campaign. Quite a woman, his Margaret.

Except of course that she wasn't his Margaret. She wasn't anyone's Margaret except her own. And she was defiantly proud of that fact.

He thought of his mother, dead these twenty years. On her death-bed she'd said, "I'm sorry, son."

"Why, ma?"

"Telling you to marry someone rich and presentable." she said with difficulty. "I thought you would be happy that way. I was wrong."

"Ma, don't worry." He'd held her gently. "Everything works out for the best. I have one of the best businesses in Colorado. I'm in the Fortune 500. I love you, ma."

"I love you, Win."

And she'd died.

Once upon a time his mother had been a strong, healthy woman whom he had always hesitated to call fat. But she was certainly "fat" by the standards of Complete Fitness. And she'd hated her own body. Year after year of dieting, followed by relapses, had compromised her immune system until she finally developed pancreatic cancer.

It had been a difficult end, and a difficult life. She had put Winston on diets from the time he was five. As a result his weight yo-yoed constantly.

Then he'd founded Complete Fitness. One of the advertisements stated that he went there every day. It was in fact true. His latest wife did, as well.

Anne, his first wife, who'd been thinner than anyone he'd known—and whom, he saw now, probably was anorexic—had never found time to come to Complete Fitness. She'd been too busy with her social whirl and not eating.

"Lovely bride," his mother had enthused.

"Hot," many of his friends had said.

Only one problem. She didn't turn him on.

He'd tried everything, including Viagra and its derivatives. Nothing. Until he'd hit on the expedient of imagining himself with Margaret when he was with Anne. When he thought of Margaret, he got hot. But when he'd shown his friends pictures of Margaret, they'd snorted, "Where'd you find the whale?" Or "You planning to marry her or take her for a ride?"

He could sympathize with his gay friends. He knew how it felt to hide your desire in the closet for years and years, never letting it out for fear of ridicule and laughter.

Anne had been the one to call it quits. "Sorry, Winston," she'd said. "I think this just isn't working." And she was right. Margaret was the type in his gut. And yes, perhaps because she reminded him of his mom. Who knew how or why people became attracted to other people?

But boy, had he flubbed it that time. She'd actually been willing to see him and what had he said? "Thin is in at parties. Fat is where it's at in bed." Oh, brilliant. She'd been right to kick him out.

Now his trophy wife Lyudmila obligingly went through all sorts of athletic moves to please him. Who wouldn't get hard when your member was taken into that mouth? But that wasn't where it really wanted to be.

There was nothing he could think of to say to make it right. He kept sending apologies through emails, notes, flowers. Most of the notes were returned. Others—perhaps she threw them out. He had no way of knowing.

The phone rang. He picked it up.

"This is Sandor Forman," the voice said. "I think we'd better talk."

Chapter 20

Amiyah & Ava

SHE WATCHED HERSELF IN PLEASURE as the advertisement came on podTV.

"GymNotTrim," the voice proclaimed as she danced, almost but not quite shedding her hip scarf. "Lose the fatigue, not the weight. Do what makes you happy!"

If what Sandor said was right, thousands of people here and millions on the Other Side were now watching her. This ad was Sandor's answer to the ad CompleteFitness was airing, the one that warned people they had better go to the gym or look like—like what? Like her? But here in FatLand ladies wanted very much to look like her.

When Ava walked into the room—she now stayed with Ava when she came to FatLand—she said, "Ava *Habibi,* I am confused."

"About what, darling?" Ava put a plate of dates and cheese in front of both of them and brought over two cups of Earl Grey to the cocktail table. Amiyah liked Earl Grey, so Ava had taken to having Earl Grey with their afternoon snack.

"On this ad—" she played the ad for Ava—"they make me lovely. But on this ad—" she played the Complete Fitness ad—"they say that people should not be like us."

"The war of the ads," Ava said. "Forman found out about the Complete Fitness ad, and he decided not to hook up with Complete Fitness after all. But in order to remain in business, in order not to lose money, he has to get more markets on the Other Side anyway. So he's appealing to people there who don't care about weight, but who think they can get sexy through exercising. Like you," she grinned, and put an arm around Amiyah.

Amiyah smiled and squeezed her hand. "So it is a war," she said. "Who will win?"

"Don't know," Ava said, putting her lips to Amiyah's neck. "But it is pretty interesting." She did not say "I hate all those people seeing you in that sexy pose," although she was thinking it. Instead she said, "And it does give some publicity to FatLand as well. You look great."

"*Shukran.*" Amiyah smiled and took off the hip scarf, as she had come close to doing but had not done in the ad.

Ava reached just below the bikini to caress Amiyah's soft, lush lower thigh. Amiyah moaned and kissed Ava on the mouth. Ava was just starting to push Amiyah down on the couch when her smartphone rang. Both of them sighed. The phone rang again.

"Can you ignore it?" Amiyah asked.

Ava sighed. "I should," she said, pushing herself up from the couch with the greatest reluctance. "And I desperately wish I could. But I can't." She answered the phone on the fourth ring. "Hello?"

"Get down here," Margaret said. "Things are happening." She paused. "Say hi to Amiyah and tell her you'll be back as soon as you can. This relates to her too, indirectly."

Ava laughed and replaced the phone. "That Margaret," she said. "Has eyes in the back of her head. She knows everything. Almost."

"When will you come back?"

"As soon as I can."

Chapter 21

Mira

MIRA SMILED as her latest date pressed his lips against hers and murmured how beautiful she was. She smiled as he kissed her good night.

She let herself into the apartment, somewhat apprehensively looking around (there had been a drunk camped outside the night before at midnight, when she'd come in from the latest ad work). FatLand didn't have that kind of drunk. In all her years there she had never heard of one, anyway. Did it have something to do with the guaranteed unemployment compensation and housing running as long as one needed them?

She sat down on the grey couch and made herself a screwdriver. Things on the Other Side were not in some ways as she had imagined.

The men who went out with her seemed to be interested in being seen with her, in going to bed with her, but not in knowing her, who she was, what she wanted, what she thought, how she responded. Granted, it was pleasant to be thought of positively, and that was why she continued to stay here. But in the atmosphere of the Pro-Health Laws, when she heard anyone making negative or nasty remarks about fat people, she found herself getting angry quickly. Once, when someone said that fat people were stupid and lazy, she retorted, "Then how come they all have bigger vocabularies than you do?"

The person, a man, laughed and said, "Oh, yeah, you were there for a while. Why?"

"I happened to be born there," she said. "My father and mother are fat, extremely intelligent, and not lazy in the least. And if you are half as intelligent as they are, you will change the subject."

Why, she wondered, *do I end up defending a place that never seemed to let me be? And how much of that was in my mind?*

But the Phys Ed teacher calling her parents was not in her mind. Nor were the giggles in study hall when she walked in.

No place completely free from bigotry, she thought. *No happy medium.*

The phone rang.

"Ms. Torelli," a woman's voice said, "this is Ava Bryer from *The FatLand Free News.*"

"Hi," she said. "How did you get my number?"

"Your parents gave it to me. They miss you a lot."

"I miss them," she said.

"Ms. Torelli," the reporter said, "did you happen to see the latest ad for GymNotTrim?"

Chapter 22

Margaret & Ava

FatLand Free News
Wednesday, March 4
A TALE OF TWO WOMEN AND TWO GYMS
BY AVA BRYER

MIRA FINISHES HER DANCE, and goes to stand near the cameraman. "How'd I do?" she asks. "Great," he says. "It's a wrap. See you tomorrow."

She heads home to her apartment in Denver. Mira, 21 years old, is slim to the point of thinness, with large dark eyes and long dark hair, an incandescent smile, and a love of movement. "I couldn't dance, couldn't exercise, couldn't even smile during my last years in FatLand," she says. "So I came here. First person to emigrate. I started out working for GymNotTrim, but then they switched their focus suddenly, so I was hired by Complete Fitness."

In response to a question about happiness, she says, "I'm not sure exactly how happy I am. But when I can enter a room and have both men and women look at me with approval, I feel free. That is what I didn't feel all those years in FatLand."

"As a matter of fact," Mira adds, "when I saw that new ad for GymNotTrim, the one with the belly dancer, I thought, 'Fine. Let them show her. She's really what they like, anyway.' What I was surprised about was that they were showing her all over the USA, on the Other Side, not just in FatLand."

Asked how she thinks people will react to their respective ads, Mira says, "I think people in FatLand will respond very positively to her ad. I know they responded really negatively to mine."

She sighs. "My parents cried; at least my mother did. But then

Complete Fitness hired me, and I told my parents how much I was getting paid. That got them quiet," she says with a hint of a chuckle.

Turning serious again, she says, "I think it's to the point where my parents realize that I'm going to have to live my own life now, apart from them, apart from FatLand. They're talking about visiting me, but that may have to wait, considering what's going on now between FatLand and here."

Amiyah, 27, is from Egypt. When asked how she feels about the respective ads for GymNotTrim and Complete Fitness, she says, "That is not surprising. But something you should know is that a lot of men on the Other Side like to look at and sleep with fat ladies, but they cannot say it. I know because when I dance on the Other Side, I get even more notes and calls than I do when I dance in FatLand."

When asked if she thinks the ad for Complete Fitness is mean-spirited, she says, "I wish people on the Other Side would know that being fat is not an illness. It is the way of the body. Some people are born fat, some are born thin. That is the way it should be. Allah makes all of us, and He is most compassionate and merciful.

"When people from FatLand see a lady telling them that they must exercise or become fat, they become very angry. When people from the Other Side see a lady dancing and telling them they don't have to lose weight, just have fun, they are shocked. They are so used to being told that they must be thinner. Now they learn that there is another way they can be."

The war between the gyms actually started out as a joint undertaking. Complete Fitness, run by Winston Stark, wanted to buy GymNotTrim and incorporate some of its practices and policies. But when FatLander Sandor Forman saw the ad featuring Mira telling people that if they didn't exercise they would wind up in FatLand, he pulled out of the deal.

The first controversy started to brew when GymNotTrim began to give out free subscriptions to its franchises in FatLand. People from FatLand felt they were being pressured to exercise, something that is prohibited by the FatLand Constitution. But now, after having seen the ads from Complete Fitness for their gyms on the Other Side, FatLanders are flocking to GymNotTrim, not necessarily to exercise, but to show loyalty to one of their own.

"I'm flabbergasted," Sandor Forman says as he sips his morning coffee. "I didn't expect this outpouring of support.

"People were pretty angry when they saw the first ad for Gym-NotTrim with Mira telling them that they would wind up in Fat-Land if they didn't exercise. I was even angrier because I hadn't been told about it. And I said something to Winston to the effect that by not telling me about the ad, and by not giving me a chance to replace it, Complete Fitness had lost a very valuable subsidiary. That was when I hired Amiyah to do the other ad, which tells people they don't have to lose weight when they are at GymNotTrim.

"What is even more amazing is that people on the Other Side seem to be responding to that ad very positively. Even a fat activist group on the Other Side who used to dislike me, FatAnd-Proud, called me and told me that as a result of the ads, more and more people on the Other Side are starting to feel that it's okay not to diet, and that it's even okay to be fat. This goes against everything they've been told for the past thirty years! And it's starting to become something more serious.

"If you'd told me last year that I and GymNotTrim would be competing successfully with Complete Fitness not only here in FatLand but on the Other Side as well, I would have asked you what drug you were taking." He stops and grins. "But now it's a reality. Our ads are out there, and we have arranged five pilot franchises on the Other Side, with ten more ready to follow if those prove successful."

Winston Stark, the CEO of Complete Fitness, was not available for comment.

IT IS IRONIC that both Stark and Forman built their gyms for similar reasons and motives. Both of them were looking for some way to stay fit, both of them were shy with girls, both of them needed confidence. Both of them built successful concerns and pioneered new, sometimes controversial, ways to reach and attract clients.

At this juncture, however, it seems that the GymNotTrim ads are drawing way more business into GymNotTrim than the Complete Fitness ads are attracting to their establishment. In FatLand, people who have seen the Complete Fitness ad (originally an ad for GymNotTrim run without the approval of Forman) are actually flocking to GymNotTrim from sheer anger at Complete Fitness.

"What do they do there if they don't exercise?" I asked Forman.

"They use the pool and the hot tubs and they eat at our excellent restaurant," he says, the grin not leaving his face. "But when someone tells them, 'Hey, you're swimming. Isn't that exercise?' they get all surprised and amazed. They were having so much fun they didn't even realize they were doing anything that could be thought of as exercise. And that's the way it should be. Why shouldn't people have fun at gyms?"

Why, indeed.

Shermaine, a member of FatAndProud on the Other Side, says, "Another way that GymNotTrim is revolutionary here is that it tells people to move and have fun and not worry about their body shapes or the way they exercise. That is what amazed and shocked people here. But they were so enthusiastic that GymNotTrim is already building franchises in areas formerly served only by Complete Fitness.

"Of course, what is even more revolutionary to some of the people here is that you can be fat and fit and not worry about what you weigh. That goes completely against the Pro-Health Laws and the weigh-ins, and what people here have been living with for years and years. We've been trying to deliver that message without success and at personal risk, since we could be arrested for it, and suddenly GymNotTrim comes along and tells people the same thing. And they start listening. It is incredible."

When asked what she thinks will happen now, Shermaine says, "I don't know, but I think it will be good. And good for fat people here and in FatLand too.

"For a long time people ridiculed anything from FatLand. Even we did. Now, with GymNotTrim, that is changing."

She laughs. "I shouldn't say this, considering our position, but more and more people are starting to ask about moving to Fat-Land as they see the ads and go to GymNotTrim. They are so positive after going to GymNotTrim that they say to themselves, 'Why can't we live this way all the time, not just when we're at the gym? Why do we have to live with the Pro-Health Laws that tell us that unless we're at the BMI of a starving population we're too heavy and have to be weighed and humiliated every week?'"

AFTER READING THE ARTICLE in the paper—she had already read it over several times before it appeared—Margaret called Ava and said, "Did you ever dream that you'd be doing a puff piece for Gym-NotTrim?"

Ava said ruefully, "I guess it ends up reading that way, doesn't it?"

"I'm teasing you," Margaret says. "It's excellent and lively and you stay out of the way when you write it, which is the ideal stance for this kind of article. And if it does get a bit enthusiastic, well, the credit goes to Forman for that. He had the sense and the vision to make incredible lemonade from lemons."

"But the amazing thing is that his lemonade may change both the USA and FatLand as we know them."

"And swell his head even more," Margaret said.

They both sighed.

"Oh well, if more people come to FatLand, we'll get more readers and you'll get promoted to Associate Editor as you should have been a year ago."

Ava laughed. "And will you start editions of *FatLand Free News* on the Other Side?"

"Don't bet that I won't."

Chapter 23

Dara

DARA TOOK A DEEP BREATH and marched into Sandor's office.

He was reading a newspaper on his smartpod, probably *The FatLand Free News,* although it could just as easily have been *The FatLand Courier Gazette.* Sandor subscribed to all three FatLand papers online.

"If you feel you have to throw me off the Board, do it," she said.

"What?" Sandor looked up. "What the hell are you talking about?

"I mean that the agency I contacted to conduct the study again did it."

"So? What did they find?"

"You won't believe it." Dara laid a sheaf of printouts on Sandor's desk.

He took a look at them, threw them down. "I can't read this medical mishmosh. Tell me what it means."

"It means that according to the latest study, FatLanders have an even higher average life expectancy than the first two studies showed, and their mortality rate is even lower than the first two studies showed."

"So we're living even longer than we thought?"

"Yes."

"So why is this a bad thing?"

"I thought you wanted—"

"I know, I know." He sighed, then reached out his hand to Dara. "I've been one hell of an unreachable bastard. That is going to change."

"Why?"

"When people on the Other Side hear that FatLand's mortality rate is even lower than we thought, and that FatLanders are even healthier than we thought, they're going to think that GymNotTrim had something to do with it. So they're going to run to us, baby."

"You were afraid previously that it would look bad if FatLand's mortality rate was consistently found to be lower than that of the Other Side."

"Yes, when I was thinking of hooking up with Complete Fitness. But now let them dance to my tune." He stood up and started to dance Dara around the room. "We're way up and they're way down."

"Congratulations," she said.

"Don't be so sarcastic," he said, stopping to touch her cheek. "We're going on a worldwide tour soon. I'm appointing someone to manage things while we take a holiday."

"I'd protest about your not consulting me," she said, "but unfortunately I've always wanted to visit Rome and Florence and the Italian countryside."

"Consider it done," he said. "Meanwhile, sit down while I start getting things in order. Or better yet, you can assist me."

"How?"

"Write down all of the places you want to see, and then find hotels that look good."

"Well," she said, "that shouldn't be too difficult."

"And when you're done," he said, "we'll go shopping and get some things we'll need. But right now—" He opened his arms. "Come here."

She held back slightly, as was always her instinct with Sandor, then went straight into his arms. "I missed you," she said. "The Sandor who stands for something. I'm so glad he's back."

"I'm glad, too," he said, kissing her.

And if stray thoughts of Alvin entered her body from time to time, she gave no sign and continued to respond enthusiastically to Sandor's lips and eyes and whispers.

Interlude

To shop for her upcoming trip, Dara went first to "My Favorite Fat Things," a thrift store and variety store specializing in secondhand and slightly unusual clothes for women. Most of the clothes were size 18 and up, but there were a few 14s and 16s. (Women size 12 and under were out of luck at this particular store.) Dara wore size 20 in most clothes, so she was right in the swim of things. The store also supplied models in one's size if one made an appointment. Since Dara wanted to see what certain swimsuits would look like on her, she had made an appointment. She watched as the model turned one way and the other, and finally decided on a black-and-white maillot and a red-and-blue flowered bikini.

"Where are you going?" the model asked. They were encouraged to be friendly with the customers.

"Italy," Dara said. "Scotland. Germany. Bulgaria. Egypt. India. Micronesia. Hawaii. Alaska."

"Oh," the model said. Her name was Stacy. "You read the FatLand Touring recommendations."

"Sure did," Dara said. "France is the worst. They throw people out for being fat. But there are so many other good places. Why worry about the bad ones?"

"How long will you be away?"

"About three months."

"Have a wonderful time."

"I sure will."

Having purchased her swimsuits, Dara browsed some of the other aisles and was pleasantly surprised to find a tan balmacaan-type rain-coat for $50. (FatLand reluctantly continued to use American currency because their economy thus far was not quite big enough for them to print and regulate their own). She grabbed it, and a long black skirt good for evening wear or day meetings when paired with a blouse or sweater. She eyed but did not buy a white angora-blend sweater, and did the same with a pair of silver sequinned leggings (neat, but where would she wear them?).

"My Favorite Fat Things" also featured fat-friendly books. Dara saw that new fiction had come in and studied the titles. She selected a new volume of erotica by one of her favorite female authors—stories pertaining to fat women who liked motorcycles and male cyclists—as well as a book of poems by a prominent fat male author. She also armed herself with *Getting the Best out of Fat Italy* and *Germany: Land of Beer, Sausages, and Zaftlicheit.*

Finally Dara gave into her desire for the red lace cami set that had beckoned her from the window. Sandor would like it, she thought. And it would be fun to prance around a hotel room in Rome wearing it.

She lunched with Sandor at Old New York, a relatively new eatery at the intersection of Ansfield Road and Wann Way.(FatLand streets were named after famous fat people and fat activists.) Since she was too excited to eat much, she settled for a corned beef on rye, which they made excellently and quite traditionally, with lots of corned beef and mustard and pickles on the side. Sandor, perhaps also a bit excited, ordered a pastrami omelet with a salad on the side. They both had the egg creams. They had found out during their first meeting that they both liked chocolate egg creams ("They're really supposed to be chocolate, not strawberry or vanilla," Sandor noted at their first meeting, and won himself a place in her heart).

"You shopped enough?" Sandor asked.

"Did you shop at all?" Dara countered.

"I did indeed." He showed her a sport jacket, denims, a pair of tan pants, a walking stick, and a Chocolate Sin kit. The sport jacket and denims, he said, had been bought at Berry's, one of the first famous clothing names to build a store in FatLand. The tan pants and walking stick came from Traveling Man, about four blocks away. The Chocolate Sin Kit—

"Chocolate Heaven," Dara giggled, naming one of FatLand's premier chocolate shops.

"Prices are hell," Sandor said, citing the line people often used in connection with the rather upscale store, "but the chocolate—"

Dara took out exactly one shoulder strap of the cami and rubbed Sandor's arm with it.

"Oho," he said, raising an eyebrow. "Watch it, missy."

Dara reinserted the strap into the bag. "Can't wait," she said.

"Neither can I."

"Bravo," she said, lifting her egg cream.

"Bravo," he echoed, lifting his.

As the sun set on Mae West Lake, they looked into each others' eyes and breathed deeply and contentedly.

Part II

Chapter 1

Amiyah

AMIYAH SMILED TO HERSELF AS She left the FatLand National Auditorium and headed to her rented car. There was a party in honor of the Best Belles' last performance this year, and she was to be honored for her work with Best Belles and for GymNotTrim. Ava was covering the party, but a few stragglers and wellwishers had held Amiyah up, or she would be with Ava now.

Amiyah clicked on the smartlock once, unlocked the car, and turned the keys. The car exploded instantly.

By the time the police and fire department arrived the fire was raging, with only the skeleton of the car visible.

WHEN AMIYAH DIDN'T REACH the party by 11:30, Ava became concerned. "Think we should call someone?" she said to Margaret.

"Probably."

Ava was about to call the police when the emcee picked up the mike and said, "I would like all of you to sit down. I am extremely sorry to have to tell you this, but there has been an explosion outside FatLand Auditorium—"

Margaret gripped Ava's hand. "Steady," she said. Ava's nails dug into Margaret's palm as she stared straight ahead. "Can you get us some water?" Margaret whispered to the person sitting next to her, an acquaintance in one of the FatLand bands.

As the emcee delivered the news, people in the audience started to scream and cry. But Ava continued to stare straight ahead, her eyes never leaving the wall above the emcee, with its FatLand flag and streamers.

Chapter 2

Reevie

IT WAS HARD TO BELIEVE, Reevie thought. Gangland style/terroristic execution in FatLand. Not only had it poisoned the air between FatLand and several Middle Eastern countries, but mothers of young women were now afraid to let them set forth alone.

Aimee and Jenna, formerly free agents at the ages of 23 and 25, now stayed home in the evening. The sad thing was that she had not even had to press them to do so. One look at the headlines, and one look at her face, and they had agreed instantly.

The grapevine felt it had something to do with GymNotTrim, and for once Reevie agreed with the grapevine, perhaps because she wanted and needed to do so. But another question was how the executioner managed to plant the explosive device so quickly and correctly. That bespoke underworld or terrorist connections.

Were we so naive, Reevie wondered, *as to think we could be free of all that? Or is it that until now we were simply insignificant enough to escape the notice of the unredeemed?*

Had the GymNotTrim ads carried more mixed blessings than they had thought? *And now we all look to our right, to our left, behind us, in front of us, around us. Several times. Paranoia does strike deep.* She hated the feeling. It was part of what she had come to FatLand all those years ago to avoid.

Someone here, Reevie thought. *Someone who was part of us. Someone who killed a wonderful and lovely dancer who brought pleasure to all who watched her. She was from another country and trusted us to create an environment safe enough to keep her from harm. And we failed.*

Reevie put on stockings and a grey tweed suit, and a black hat with a brim to signal her mourning for Amiyah. There was a Board meeting tonight. She wondered if it would help anything. But of course it was very necessary.

She called to Aimee and Jenna, "I'm leaving now. Please don't open the door and don't answer the house phone."

"Okay, Ma," they said together, sounding grumpy.

Reevie sighed and dialed Alvin's smartphone number to let him know she was on her way.

Chapter 3

The FatLand Board

Ed Torelli looked slowly around the room. He knew all the members were present, but he wished to make their presence a little larger than life. After all, the media were covering the meeting tonight; recent occurrences and shocks had catapulted official FatLand gatherings into events.

"I would like to request at this time that we all stand to honor Amiyah in a moment of silence."

All the Board members and media people stood.

After a minute, Ed said, "All those who wish to say a few words about Amiyah may now do so."

As they knew she would, Ava walked up to the microphone. Margaret looked at her to give her encouragement.

"Amiyah," Ava started. "You were a bringer of light and life. You swam into our lives bringing pleasure and your sunny personality. Born in the sun, you brought the best of your culture and brought out the best in all of us. We will miss you always."

She stopped. It seemed to those seated that she was thinking of saying more, but she replaced the mike and went back to her seat on the sidelines.

Reevie took the mike next. "Amiyah," she said, "you delighted us with your dancing and your skill. You smiled on us all. And we paid you back by not guarding you while someone arranged to have you killed. Your triumph remains with you, but our shame remains with us. If your soul is with us, please know that we will not rest until we find out how and why it was catapulted so suddenly into the next world.

We miss you. And we intend to do right by you."

A few Board and media members were crying quietly by now. Ed took the mike. "Amiyah," he said. "We've lost a wonderful dancer and a good friend. You showed people the best of us and what we could be, given the chance. Even though you left us because someone forced you to, your contributions to life and health and hope here will not be forgotten. I do not say goodbye because I hope that many of us will meet you again eventually. But I do say *'Salaam Aleikum,'* friend. Thank you for being with us as long as you were. Bless you in all worlds."

The crying grew more widespread. Ed said, "We will take a minute to collect ourselves. Then we will move onto the business before the Board tonight."

Some took deep breaths. Others took tissues. The room grew quiet again.

Ed nodded at all, then stood up again. "Does everyone here have copies of the agenda for tonight?" He looked around the room. All nodded or sat quietly. "Good." He circled the room with his eyes, then started again. "The first item on the agenda is indeed Amiyah's demise. We have set up an investigative committee with police liaisons in both FatLand and the Other Side. We have two private detectives who are contributing their services as well. One resides in FatLand, the other over the border in Colorado. I would like to introduce them to you."

From the nodding and general buzz greeting his announcement, Ed saw that many of the Board and onlookers found it comforting that Detective Sergeant Ron Leffler was fat. Joann whispered to Reevie that he reminded her of Perry Mason.

Leffler resided in FatLand. The Colorado detective was short and thin and quiet. The Board would receive updates on Amiyah's case via smartmail every week, and more often if they wished.

Alvin was handling the medical part along with the pathologist and the coroner. He introduced his colleagues to the Board. He had smartmailed Dara, who was now in Italy.

The next item came as a surprise to most of the Board members and as a shock to most of the onlookers.

"Usually at this time of year we focus on budgetary concerns," Ed said. "However, today I am preempting the budget discussion for an item of grave importance that has just come to my attention." He looked at the smartpod. "I wish to inform this meeting that Stark Enterprises, of which Complete Fitness is a component, is officially suing GymNotTrim, of which Sandor Forman is the CEO, for reneging on its agreement to merge with Complete Fitness."

"Oh my God." Margaret clutched Ava.

"Steady," Ava said to Margaret. It was now her turn to comfort, or at least calm. "Let's hear what and when the bastard is lowering the boom."

"Sandor Forman," Ed continued, "is requested to appear before the Colorado 4th Circuit Court, which includes Denver, on March 25th."

"He knows, doesn't he?" Alvin said.

"Oh yes," Ed said. "He knows."

"He's using Hobson Bates, his usual firm, right?" Ava said.

"I assume so," Ed said.

"What can we do to help?" Joann asked.

"Publicize it here and on the Other Side as much as possible," Margaret said. "It's not difficult. A lot of people on the Other Side were starting to join GymNotTrim after—" She stopped, looking quickly at Ava. "Well, they really appreciated their approach."

"He and Dara will have to cut short their trip," Alvin said. "Damned shame."

Reevie looked quickly at Alvin as he said that, but his eyes were neither excited nor dreamily intent. Relieved, she took a quick breath and said, "They got the chance to go through Italy, though. That's the best part."

"Indeed it is," Margaret agreed.

Alvin smiled and said to Reevie, "One day we'll go there, darling."

"One day when you start believing in vacations," she said, her words cross, her heart light.

The rest of the Board members laughed.

Chapter 4

Dara & Sandor

"I'VE PHONED FOR A TAXI," Dara told Sandor. She continued to gaze out the window over the warm hills of Abruzie.

"How long?"

"Fifteen minutes."

"I'm packed."

"So am I." Dara inhaled the fragrances of the field along with the new construction whining on the other side of the hotel. "I hope we can come back someday."

"Sure," Sandor agreed, but without much conviction.

"Oh come on, San, he can't do anything."

"Probably not," Sandor agreed, "but he can make things damned difficult. He can tie us up for months on end. That's probably what he had in mind, anyway."

"Well, I am sure your lawyers will get us out of it."

"It's going to be his lawyers versus our lawyers," Sandor said, "and frankly, I'm not sure who will win."

Dara sighed. "Any news about Amiyah?"

"No." He looked somber. "That will take a long time, I think."

"Do you think Stark did it?"

"It's so obvious. Did he really think he could get away with it?"

"You're sure he did it? Not a jealous boyfriend? Or girlfriend?" Dara added.

"Ava worshipped her. She would tear whoever touched her limb from limb."

"Yeah," Dara agreed. "Everyone loved her. So why—?"

"Makes sense for it to be Stark."

"Yes. Too much sense."

Dara took one final look out the window. "Okay," she said. "I'm ready. Guess we better go down."

"Yeah," Sandor agreed. He rang for a bellhop. "At least we had this."

"Yes." She grabbed her purse. It shone white against her newly tanned skin. "Do you have the entrance card?"

"We just leave it here, I think. They'll pick it up later."

"Right."

Chapter 5

Sandor

The trial of Sandor Forman for reneging on his agreement to merge GymNotTrim with Complete Fitness is scheduled to begin in the 4th Circuit Court of Colorado...

THE FATLAND FREE NEWS, March 21

AS SANDOR WALKED UP THE STAIRS of the courthouse, he realized he had forgotten what life on the Other Side was like.

He saw lots of hungry-looking angry people, very few of whom were very thin. They seemed to crowd in on all sides. Suddenly they began to chant.

"FatLand no! FlatLand yes!"

Some called out "Fat slob! Fat slob!" which astounded him, since he was immaculately attired in an Italian suit, white shirt, and discreetly printed silk tie. Yes, he had gained weight in the past few years, but he had continued to go to GymNotTrim faithfully, sometimes for the sheer fun of it.

The chants continued. "Don't bring us your flab! Squeeze into a cab!"

A thin reporter caught up with him at the top of the stairs. "Whoa, whoa," he puffed. "Can't keep up with you, Mr. Forman. So how does it feel living without chocolate and cake and candy and pie?"

"I don't eat cake and candy and pie," Sandor said. "I prefer cheese and meat sandwiches."

"Cheese and meat are available in one ounce portions," the reporter intoned.

"I know," Sandor agreed. "Pro-Health Laws of 2012. Maybe I'll get some later. Now I'm focusing on the matter at hand."

"How does it feel to carry around all that excess weight?" another reporter shouted.

"Excess compared to what?" Sandor said. "If we live longer and easier and happier lives than you do, what is excessive about that?"

"Everyone knows those mortality numbers were cooked," the reporter yelled.

"You're right," Sandor said. "The first study was not correct. Turned out that it actually underestimated the gap. Our third study showed that FatLanders live on average 2 to 4 years longer than Other Siders." He purposely used the somewhat derogatory FatLand term for people living outside FatLand.

"Stark says you were afraid that Complete Fitness would give Fat-Landers negative feelings about their body image," the first reporter said.

"I think he was more afraid that GymNotTrim was giving Other Siders positive images about theirs," Sandor shot back.

"Go to hell, you fatso," the second reporter shouted.

"From what I can see, you're all living there already," Sandor replied as he entered the 4th Circuit Courthouse.

The Colorado Sun-Journal carried this headline at noon: FORMAN CALLS COLORADO HELL.

THE BOARD, who had elected to watch the proceedings on Alvin and Reevie's amphitheater screen, all laughed as they watched the noon news. Dara laughed along with them. "Give 'em hell, Sandor," Alvin yelled as they clapped.

Only when she was alone in the Johnsons' beautiful bathroom with the marble jacuzzi and swimtub did Dara allow herself to cry.

Chapter 6

Jesse

JESSE WOKE UP, as usual, around 8 AM.

He was in college—FatLand Technical College. He was writing his Senior Honors Thesis on "The Biometrics of Bus Seating in FatLand," which discussed the history of how FatLand Founders had engaged a biometrics expert to figure out how wide and long to make the seats in FatLand buses, and where to put the seats on long distance and commuter FatLand bus lines. It was an interesting study and until recently had engaged much of his attention.

Some of his attention had also centered on the FatLand Tech football team, for which he played guard. The most fun of all for him had been to ram a guard from the Other Side.

When the Pro-Health Laws of 2012 had been passed football teams—both college and professional—on the Other Side had been so severely affected that many of them had gone to FatLand. A few had gone to Canada and to Hawaii, which, along with Alaska, mostly sidestepped the Pro-Health Laws. This resulted in FatLand suddenly possessing a wealth of football talent. Many who could not continue playing because of the sheer numbers of footballers found work at GymNotTrim.

The Other Side still fought to maintain football teams, which mostly played each other. But when any of them came to FatLand, they suffered severely. Not because they were that much lighter, but because they lacked the energy of the FatLand teams, which were not forbidden any foods. Thus Jesse exulted—or had exulted—in being able to tackle Other Side guards and have them go down easily, especially after teams from the Other Side called FatLand teams "puffballs" and "fatties" in the press.

In the past two weeks Jesse had missed several practice sessions, however, a fact that would have alarmed his parents had they known. But they didn't know. *Easygoing Jesse,* he thought. *They always assume everything is okay with me because I fall so easily into FatLand life. In so many ways I'm exactly what FatLanders are supposed to be. Like a poster guy.* And indeed Jesse's face and build adorned many an ad for FatLand Tech.

But since Mira had started doing those ads for GymNotTrim and then for Complete Fitness, he had suffered continuous and sometimes vicious teasing. "How's Skinny Minnie?" a teammate said. "Is she still strutting her stuff?" Or "What's up with the thin slut?"

Jesse had threatened to slug the guy, who had stopped for a while— a beating from muscular, superstrong Jesse was not a prospect to be taken lightly. But he then started up again, as teasers and bullies did. Of course in FatLand high schools they had an excellent program enforced against bullying of any kind. But this guy had transferred from a university on the Other Side. (Jesse wondered briefly if this policy of letting Other Siders transfer into FatLand colleges and universities was wise.) He supposed he could see the counseling service. But damn it, the bully needed counseling, not him!

As members of the FatLand Board, his parents were preoccupied these days with efforts to find the killer of Amiyah and with giving support to Sandor Forman, who was on trial on the Other Side for going back on his agreement to merge with Complete Fitness. They seemed, he thought with some anger, to have given up on Mira.

But he hadn't. In the quiet of his room he prepared some books to send to her and scanned some photos that he would later send to her pod. He missed her very much, even though he knew she was probably happier on the Other Side.

He thought briefly of Amiyah, the dancer who had been killed, but didn't like to think about that more than necessary. Thinking about her—and those ads in which she danced—started things in him he couldn't name and didn't wish to keep.

He continued to wrap the books he was sending Mira, hoping she would like them.

Chapter 7

Sergeant Leffler

SERGEANT LEFFLER was perplexed.

Over the last year FatLand had had two instances of stealing, three manhandlings (not assaults), five instances of littering and seven arguments between neighbors. As far as he knew, there were no gangs, no syndicates, not even any organized youth rivalries.

He sent two able junior grade detectives to check and recheck contacts to make sure no hidden gangland activities were occurring. When they returned, they reported that they could find no evidence of gangland activity in FatLand.

Since there were no jails in FatLand, there were also no cases of recidivism or jail-based gangs.

"Ergo," Sergeant Leffler said to his junior grade detectives, "we have to find out if anyone from outside with gangland contacts somehow managed to sneak in without our being aware of it. That means going through all the entrance papers and podscanning, then podmailing them to Detective Vance on the Other Side."

So for about an hour they scanned in the first pages of passports, then sent the names to Detective Carl Vance. In half an hour, Detective Vance podmailed back, "No gangland connections detected."

"This means one of two things," Sergeant Leffler said. "Either someone from the Other Side without a record was purposely sent in here to do the work of some syndicate or gang. Or—it's someone from here."

He and the junior grade detectives sifted through names and ages and sent ten that he thought might possibly be interested in working for syndicates on the Other Side. He podmailed Detective Vance and explained what they were looking for. Half an hour later, Detective Vance podmailed back, "Investigations complete. No known possibilities of gangland connections."

"In that case," Sergeant Leffler said, "we've got to face the unfaceable. It was done by someone from here."

"But who would—?" one of the junior grade detectives asked. "And why?"

"That," Sergeant Leffler said, "is what we have to find out."

"How?" the other junior grade detective said.

"We have to figure out why someone from here would want to kill her. But we can narrow it down a bit. It would have to be someone who knew how to make the crime resemble a gangland murder."

"So Stark doesn't come into this at all?"

"Not that we can see."

"But who would be able to make it look like a gangland murder?"

"Someone with some kind of background. Science, explosives, physics, that sort of thing."

"A professional scientist?"

"Maybe."

"But why—?"

"Why," Sergeant Leffler said, "is the cousin of how, when, and where. Not to mention who."

He continued, "How? Explosives. When? At night. Where—empty theater parking lot. So we have someone who is obviously mobile, old enough to be out and about, also someone who knew how to set remote detonation devices. Someone who might or might not have given some clue before this happened."

"Can we learn anything from the Net?"

"Good question. Time to visit the FatLand sites. And the blogs."

"But there are hundreds, maybe thousands."

"That," Sergeant Leffler said, "is why we are going to start looking now."

Chapter 8

Joann & Reevie

JOANN CALLED Reevie. "There's something I think needs looking into by the Board, but I wanted to run it by you first. I wanted all the drama out of the way first. Sandor should really be here too, but—"

"Shoot."

"Well, I do financial reports for various FatLand institutions, as you know."

"So formal," Reevie said. "Come on, Jo, spill it."

"The FatLand National Bank recorded no intra-territory spending in the last quarter."

"What?"

"You heard me. It was flat. Zero. Nada. Zilch."

"That's impossible."

"That's what I said. So I called Trudy. She's the Bank Officer I report to when I'm doing the reports."

"And?"

"She said they'd look the data over again."

"And did they?"

"She never got back to me."

"Did you call her again?"

"Yep. A week ago."

"And?"

"Nothing."

"Did you tell this to Ed?"

"Yes."

"What did he say?"

"He said there might be a possible conflict of interest, since I'm on the Board and I am the one doing their financial report."

"I don't see that there would be," Reevie said. "For one reason: You are not an employee of the bank. You're an independent contractor. You handle other reports."

"But theoretically I could have an interest in how the report turns out."

"How?"

"If I wanted to sell the results. Actually I'm forbidden by contract from disclosing the results."

"Well, if that's the case, you can't very well go to the Board with this without problems. But I'm wondering if there might be another way to get this resolved."

"If you can think of it," Joann said, "please tell me. It's been on my mind for a while, but I didn't know quite where to take it."

"Is it okay if I talk to Alvin?"

"Sure."

What You Need To Know About Living in FatLand

(brochure handed to people who choose to emigrate
from other countries/states to FatLand)

There is no unemployment in FatLand.

Every FatLander is assigned an Employment Counselor. It is up to the individual to contact the Employment Counselor when and where and for however long she or he wishes. Some people become friendly with their Employment Counselor and check in regularly. Others don't see their Employment Counselor at all.

What the Employment Counselor does is, first of all, assist an individual who wishes to relocate, retrain, or revitalize her or his career or occupation. Some may wish to utilize this service extensively; others may feel that they do not need it.

In FatLand no one is discriminated against on the basis of weight or looks. Thus we are able to utilize the talents of our citizens to the fullest. We are also able to maintain a steady surplus because all of our citizens contribute to the tax base.

Taxes in FatLand are as follows.

- People earning less than $1 million dollars per year do not pay taxes.

- People earning between $1 million and $2 million dollars pay from 3 to 7 percent of their gross income.

- People earning between $3 million and $4 million pay between 7 to 10 percent.

- The scale escalates until, at $100 million per year, 25 percent is paid.

However, it should be noted that there are *absolutely no loopholes allowed.* No trusts, no capital gains.

Retirement funds are adminstered and financed by a combination of government agencies and employers. Upon retirement, every FatLander receives both a lump sum, to be invested as she or he sees fit, and a pension.

Healthcare is paid for entirely by the Government of Fat-Land.

Chapter 9

Reevie & Joan

TWO DAYS LATER, Reevie called Joann.

"I spoke to Alvin," she said. "About the lack of intra-territorial spending."

"And?"

"He thinks you should tell the Board anyway."

"Even though it might be a conflict of interest?"

"Alvin said that the Board does oversee the Bank, after all."

"I have an idea," Joann said. "Have the Board meeting. Bring it up. But I won't attend this time. Then at least it comes from someone else."

"That's a thought," Reevie agreed. "Haven't heard from Trudy?"

"Not a thing."

"Another idea," Reevie said. "The Bank presents the Board with quarterly reports. Wouldn't this item show up?"

"Not necessarily."

"Why not?"

"Because I'm not sure that intra-territorial spending shows up as a separate item. It's pretty much subsumed under Government spending."

"But it would be Bank spending, wouldn't it?"

"A lot of the sources are governmental, though."

"So it wouldn't show up?"

"It might not."

"All right," Reevie said. "We'll have the meeting. For formality's sake. Then we'll send an official Board letter to Trudy. How's that?"

"Only one problem," Joann said. "How would you justify your knowing about the irregularity?"

"We can say we received it on a preliminary report. And I'll bet no one is going to say, 'Oh, that isn't itemized—how can you know about that?'"

Joann said, "That's a load off my mind. At least I don't feel so isolated."

"You shouldn't feel that way," Reevie said. "There's something fishy somewhere. We have to figure it out."

Chapter 10

Ava

Ava LOOKED IN CONFUSION around the room, then stopped the alarm and looked at the time. 6:20 AM. Ten more minutes and she would have to get up. Strangely enough, she was so interested in what she was covering—and uncovering—that she did not even want to go back to sleep.

And she had been so reluctant to take the assignment.

"It'll take your mind off a lot of things," Margaret had said. "And you get to stay free."

"Gee, can't turn it down, then."

"Come on," Margaret said. "You're the best reporter we have. I can't give this to anyone else."

"Hmm, but I wish it were anyone except Sandor. Why don't you take it instead? I could hold down the fort here."

"You know why I can't take it."

"Yes. I know."

So here she was, getting into the shower, which seemed way too small. She was discovering anew just how difficult it had been to live on the Other Side, since FatLand stipulated a shower and bathroom size that was a lot more generous than this cupboard—or so she put it to herself.

The room was also too small, she was finding. As a matter of fact, everything seemed small, somehow—the court, the streets, the markets, but especially the people. If they had all been thin, she would have understood. The strange thing was that they were not all thin, but they seemed—well, short. Could the stipulations of the Pro-Health

Laws have caused people on the Other Side to shrink in height?

Time for her morning coffee and breakfast. Oh, she'd forgotten. Coffee had been forbidden, although she didn't quite see why. She made non-caffeined tea instead in the pot provided by the hotel. She thought instinctively of rolls and bagels and croissants, but then remembered that the only bread-like product available was whole wheat. Lowfat yogurt and fruit were the other choices. *They must save a bundle on menus,* she thought, laughing to herself.

She stopped. It was the first time since—well, since that night that she had laughed. It hurt again because she felt it was not yet time to laugh. She lapsed into quiet sadness, which the non-caffeined tea did not help.

Where was that one place that served outlawed things like cream cheese and pies and eggs? Reevie had told her about it, since it was there that she met with members of FatAndProud, whom Ava was to contact that night. Well, maybe then she would be able to eat like a human being. Until that time—

Ava ordered two pieces of whole wheat toast and fruit. "You can skip the yogurt," she told room service. No doubt they were shocked that a FatLander would pass up an entire course. But she never had liked yogurt, and she felt lowfat yogurt would not improve her opinion.

The whole wheat toast came with the latest lowfat derivative. Amazing. Scientists and nutritionists had disproved the fat-disease/illness connection twenty years ago, and yet the Other Side clung to the outdated, outmoded diet stipulated by those archaic Pro-Health Laws.

If they're so concerned about nutrition, they should research all these fat substitutes they slop onto their food, Ava thought as she scraped the stuff off. She bit into the now-dry toast and continued to drink her her non-caffeined tea.

AFTER THE LESS-THAN-SATISFYING BREAKFAST, Ava dressed with especial care. She put on a black suit with a white shirt and shined black shoes, and pulled her hair back in a ponytail. She picked up her bag and went outside.

Not a bad day for March, she thought. A little cool, but still sunny. She started to walk the six blocks to the courthouse.

Cars passed by, but rather slowly, since it was rush hour. The drivers gawked and yelled "Fat bitch!" A few screamed "Fat dyke! " Which shocked her. But when she arrived at the courthouse, she understood why. All of the women—reporters, audience, jury—were wearing skirts.

Strange, she thought. Had pants gone out of style for women? She would have to ask the members of FatAndProud that night. Well, she wasn't about to change her style of dress in early, cold spring just for Other Siders.

Luckily she was spared the indignity of the small courtroom seats and the hostile audience. Reporters now had cubicles from which they could report to their home audiences without being heard by anyone in the Court.

She began, "I'm standing here in a cubicle in the 4th District Colorado State Court, in Denver, Colorado, in the United States of America, known to many of you as the Other Side. In about ten minutes, the second day of the trial of Sandor Forman, citizen of FatLand and very successful owner of the GymNotTrim enterprise, will begin.

"As many of you may know, the first day of the trial, yesterday, established that Sandor Forman did indeed renege on his agreement to merge his company with that of Complete Fitness, owned by Winston Stark and Associates. What Sandor's lawyers—Halston and Bates, whom many of you know—will seek to establish today is the reason for his reneging.

"As I stand here, I can see the audience seating themselves. Now the lawyers for Mr. Forman are walking in, along with Mr. Forman himself. The judge, Judge Dearing Stolworthy, has arrived and is walking in slowly.

"Finally Mr. Winston Stark, followed by his lawyers, is strolling in. The judge is assuming his robes. The sergeant-at-arms is motioning for us to rise.

"The second day of the trial of Complete Fitness versus GymNotTrim is about to begin. More when we have all been seated."

Trial Into Second Day;
Colorado tries to pin down Forman
by Ava Bryer

THE COURTROOM IS SOMBER, almost gloomy in the early spring that is still winter here in Colorado. The audience matches it in black and navy apparel, as if they had all been informed that uniforms were necessary.

In stark contrast to the Coloradoans, Forman sits in his tan suit, white shirt, and Italian silk tie. He nods occasionally as his lawyer whispers to him.

Winston Stark seems to hover above the proceedings like an evil angel in his dark funereal suit, his glance betraying amusement and anger by turn. He has not yet spoken, since Forman has been on the bench for two days and his lawyers have not yet had a chance to cross-question Stark.

Ordinarily this would be a cut-and-dried case. Colorado law stipulates that for a business contract to be rescinded, it must be voided in the first week after signing. FatLand sees it differently; Contracts can be nullified at any time if it can be proven that one of the partners was not consulted about any part of the enforcement of the contract. If this were FatLand, Forman would have a strong case.

But it is not FatLand. Today Stark's lawyers tried to get Forman to admit that he wished to void the contract because he was not getting enough say in GymNotTrim after the merger. Forman, on the other hand, kept harping on the fact that Complete Fitness was actually taking an approach that would have destroyed GymNotTrim. This, he intimated, may have been Stark's objective in the first place, instead of the increased business from GymNotTrim franchises that would have merged with Complete Fitness.

Stark's lawyers kept managing to voice objections that were often sustained by the judge. This, of course, would be counter to FatLand law, which states that lawyers cannot object to answers to their own questions. The judge admonished Forman to "stick to the subject at hand" and told the court recorder to strike a few of his answers from the record. But Forman succeeded in placing his doubts into not only the heads of the jury, but the many Other Siders and FatLanders watching the trial on video.

When the day's proceedings concluded, some Coloradoans interviewed by reporters said they had gone to GymNotTrim franchises in the past month since they had opened up on the Other

Side, and that they really appreciated the idea of being able to exercise without worrying about losing weight.

But it turns out that the thing that made and makes Gym-NotTrim so popular among Other Siders is not the philosophy, but the food. GymNotTrim serves snacks and even entrees that are outlawed in Colorado. There is nothing in Colorado law or even the Pro-Health Laws to prevent imported food from being served at GymNotTrim, whose primary classification is as a gym, not a restaurant.

This of course did not prevent Stark from trying to get new additions to the Pro-Health Laws passed. However, certain Coloradoan size acceptance groups, such as FatAndProud, were instrumental in stopping him from ramming such changes through. Thus Stark deployed his next strategy, which was to take Forman to court for reneging on his contract.

In front of the courthouse, it is possible to see only demonstrators and supporters for "FreedomFit," a group paid for by Stark. They allegedly believe it is not possible to be healthy without conforming to the weights published by First Colorado Insurance, on whose board Stark sits as well. Ironically, Stark, who is not extremely thin but possesses a good covering of muscles, would probably be over these prescribed weights himself.

FatAndProud applied for a permit to demonstrate outside the courthouse, but was refused.

Tomorrow Forman's lawyers will question Stark about why he decided to wait for three weeks before taking Forman to court for reneging on the contract.

Chapter 11

Detective Vance on the Other Side, in Colorado

An admitted surfing addict, Detective Vance still liked desktops in an age in which Pods of all kinds ruled. He knew surfers these days did their thing on huge flat screens with interactive video offerings (he remembered it used to be called "TV"), but his upgraded and souped-up Eftron did what he liked best—delivered the best speed in the most comfortable manner possible (Vance liked it best when he could surf on Sunday mornings with a bagel and coffee. Alas, the bagel had to be whole wheat and the cream cheese nonfat since the passage of the Pro-Health Laws, and lox of course was completely forbidden, but he gamely kept his routine.)

Detective Sergeant Leffler had mailed him the results of their blog and net search on FatLand sites—seemingly nil. There was simply nothing that was in any way dangerous, violent, or explosive. Vance himself chalked it up to people staying in good moods because they were allowed to eat anything they wanted (he sighed and remembered cocoa, as well). He mailed Leffler back that he would do as much searching as he could and see if he got the same results.

As Leffler had done, Vance first searched the FatLand sites and blogs. He was forced to conclude that there was simply nothing there that would yield any clues. No one seemed angry or intent on destroying anything, unless it was nonfat milk or (he had to laugh) nonfat yogurt and cream cheese. He tried a series of searches using "Fat" and "Land" in different applications. Still nothing.

He opened the window and peered out. Spring was late this year and the snow was falling again. He was also following the Forman trial, and he decided almost idly to survey sites and blogs that commented on it mainly as a break from his previous search. He was surfing such blogs when he clicked on one called "Chewing the Fat."

He read its mission statement: "This blog is for like minds who think fat people should be boiled, roasted and drained slowly. Then they should be fed to pets. Long live the Thin Homeland!"

Vance gaped.

The blog's commentary on the Forman trial went as follows: "FatSlob Forman (Forman really didn't look that fat to Vance, and certainly no fatter than many Coloradoans) wants to peddle his slimy ideas about not losing weight to Thin Homelanders. After the judge throws the book at him (which we think is a foregone conclusion), we hope that he is thrown into a Thin Homeland prison to feed the rats. Come to think of it, there is too much fat on him to feed Thin Homeland rats, who prefer lean meat, not that glop that FatLanders have on their nonexistent bones."

Vance shuddered. One reason he himself hadn't married is that he liked heavy women, but it would have been a death knell to his career on the Other Side to be seen married to one.

The blog was violent, fascist, brutal, all the things one associated with fringe activities. If someone with the feelings encapsulated in the blog had seen Amiyah on TV—and it was more than possible that they had—it was certainly also possible that someone connected in some way with the blog might have decided to knock her off.

But the style of the killing was that of organized crime, not of angry bloggers, even those with fascist tendencies. And all evidence pointed to the fact that the killing had been an inside job.

And yet—

Vance podmailed his junior grade detectives the link to the blog and told them to have a look at it. He then podmailed Leffler and said to him, "Take a look at this. I know it doesn't match exactly what we were looking for, but it set some bells ringing in my mind. See what you think."

Chapter 12

Sergeant Leffler

SERGEANT LEFFLER GAZED at the "Chewing the Fat" blog in fascination and disgust. It was the kind of thing that someone on the Other Side would come up with, he figured, although he hadn't thought to track blogs like it previously.

As did Detective Vance, he noted the hatred, the brutal fascism, the anger, but at first he didn't see how such a blog might relate to the murder or even to people in FatLand, since it originated on the Other Side, and there had been no entries or exits from FatLand around the time of the murder. And yet his mind couldn't let go.

He summoned his junior grade detectives and showed them the blog. He could have simply podmailed the site to them, but he felt a meeting might encourage input and ideas.

Sure enough, JGD Sandra Fairlane looked at the blog and said, "Powerful stuff in its way. I wouldn't want my kids to see it."

Sergeant Leffler looked at her, and then around the room. JGD Don Milstein said, "How do we know that none of them did?"

"My God," JGD Flores said, her dark eyes snapping. "If any kids here saw this—"

"We can check," JGD Kumar Singh said.

Sergeant Leffler said, "Let's do that right now."

Half an hour later he podmailed Detective Vance: "16 FatLand ISPs located that accessed this blog; 10 access it regularly. We're going into the field to ask some questions."

He divided up the ten regular accessor ISPs. Each would take two. "Report back here as soon as you're finished," he said.

Chapter 13

Ava

AVA LOOKED WITH SOME TREPIDATION at the peeling facade of The Laurels diner and the faded sign under the old-fashioned flashing neon. *If ever there were a venue for something shady,* she thought—

But when she got inside she saw six members of FatAndProud sitting at a table in the middle of the room. Two stood as she entered.

"Hey," she said, and extended her hand.

"Good to see you," two of the members said. The others smiled.

She saw the menus and picked one up. "Wow," she said. "Pretty nice, even compared to us."

"Everyone comes here sometimes," Paula, who was short, with red hair and a fringed pine-green pants suit, said. "They just don't tell."

"How's Reevie?" Shermaine asked.

"She's good," Ava said. "Strong, happy. She's fine."

They gave their orders. The waitress, a thin grumpy-looking woman in her sixties, actually smiled when Ava said, "I'd like the Chocolate Cloud Castle."

"Excellent choice," she beamed.

"You doing a story on us?" Tammy asked.

"One of the feature stories of the series," Ava said, as the thought came to her out of nowhere that she would loved to come here with Amiyah. Tears came to her eyes. *That's how it goes,* she thought. *I'm fine, then suddenly—*

Ricki, who saw the tears said, "Hey, are you okay?"

"Sure," Ava said. "Just a reaction to dust or something in the air, I think." She wiped her eyes with a tissue and hoped no more tears would surface. "I really wanted to write about you folks. I'm really proud of the work you do."

"It might be dangerous," Annie said. She was tall and blond and wore a royal blue skirt set with white boots.

"Why?"

"Because there's a lot of fallout from the trial right now."

"How?" Ava asked, and leaned forward.

"They're saying that FatLanders want to take over Colorado and other parts of the USA. Because of GymNotTrim. Then they look at us and yell 'Go to FatLand where you belong!'"

"Sometimes they do more," Shermaine said.

The other members nodded and Paula said, "Tell her, Shermaine."

"On my house," Shermaine said. "In white paint. 'Die, fat nigger wench.'"

"Tell her the rest," Annie said.

"Someone left a message on my VoicePod. 'Your kind doesn't belong here. Leave or face the consequences.'"

"What did they mean by 'your kind'?" Ava asked. "Great, the way in a crisis this place regresses 200 years."

"Ava," Ricki said, "the atmosphere has gotten really strange here. For years we were taunted about our size, especially after the Pro-Health Laws. But now—it's as if we're infected with a really horrible disease, and they're trying to quarantine us."

"But at the same time, everyone comes here," Ava says. "And consumes these amazing creations. Reminds me of the societies where homosexual activity was once forbidden, but so many people paid to do it on the sly."

"Yes," Annie said. "But it seems to be getting worse than mere hypocrisy. It's combined with hatred now. There's a blog that came out recently. It's called 'Chewing the Fat.' It advocates cannibalizing fat people. We're hoping it's supposed to be some sick joke."

"So the hatred grows," Ava said.

"It's gotten to the point where—" Paula stopped. "We've been wondering if we could claim asylum in FatLand."

Ava sighed. "You could," she said. "And they would be glad to have you. But what about all the fat people here who need help standing up for their rights? Everyone admired you for that. You were heroes to all of us in FatLand."

"We don't want to be dead heroes," Shermaine said. "Here." She pushed a Pod to Ava. "Take a look at that."

FAT AND PROUD IN THE LAND OF THIN-WORSHIP
BY AVA BRYER

ANNIE TURNS TO GREET another member of FatAndProud as they both walk into that restaurant—everyone knows the one—in Colorado where people come to eat "real food."

"Even we don't eat this kind of food most of the time," Annie says as they order. "We can't because of the Pro-Health Laws. Our ID cards tell them exactly how much we've bought, and where. This place circumvents that by keeping it cash only. It's a complete anachronism, but so is the food. Sometimes I wonder how many people in this wonderful land of ours are starving, and not because they are poor, but because the USA passed laws that keep people hungry."

"The worst part," Shermaine says, tucking into steak and a potato with sour cream, "is that people here think we must be breaking the Pro-Health Laws. And yet we don't eat anymore than anyone else these days. We can't. We eat when we come here. Period. And plenty of thin people come to this restaurant, I can assure you."

Paula, short and curvy with a glorious mane of red hair, says, "It's not even particular foods that I miss." She starts on her salmon croquettes. "It's knowing that I can have anything I want when I want it." Then she laughs. "Actually, people are starting to find that when they go to GymNotTrim, they can also have food like this. Hmm, not sure if I'm allowed to say that."

"Why not?" Ricki says. "The law doesn't forbid us from talking about food. We're not supposed to want it, but everyone does, anyway."

THIS IS THE THEME of FatAndProud's latest newsletter: "Food, Glorious Food: Will It Take Another Revolution?"

"What kind of revolution?" Ricki says upon being asked. "Hopefully a very tasty one." She laughs.

"In the atmosphere these days, no one has yet come to take us away. But there are at least ten thousand people in prison for breaking the Pro-Health Laws. Can you imagine? Ten thousand people guilty of nothing except selling or buying more food than they were 'allowed' to, or food that had too much dairy or fat or sugar content.

"This, by the way, is twenty years after studies proved that fat content had nothing to do with getting any diseases. We keep wondering how long it's going to take for the American people to get wise to the Big Diet Industry that pushed through these laws, and to rebel against them.

"We keep campaigning for anti-discrimination laws for fat people, and sometimes we are successful. But the main crux of the problem is that too many people—fat and thin and middling—feel bad and hungry and tired all the time, too tired to rebel.

"I think Big Diet is afraid that if the Pro-Health Laws were repealed, they would be next. And no one would ever go on a diet again." She laughs.

Tammy says, "Sticking together makes us feel better because each of us knows that we're not the only one. But the atmosphere lately has taken a turn for the worse. We've gotten more hate messages in the past month than we've had for the past twenty years."

Upon being asked if this has to do with the current trial against GymNotTrim, most of them nod. Shermaine says, "It definitely has to do with that. See, GymNotTrim not only doesn't stress diet, but it stresses fun. And the same people who want people not to get any pleasure out of food also don't want them to get any pleasure out of anything else. They hate the idea of lots of happy people—slim and fat—walking around contented, full and friendly. Then they wouldn't be able to sell people things by making them feel dissatisfied with themselves or their bodies."

"But don't the Pro-Health Laws sort of preclude that?" I can't help asking. "If people can't eat more than a certain amount per day, and of certain foods only, how can they feel dissatisfied with themselves in that area?"

"You've seen the ads for Complete Fitness," Paula says. "Somehow they still manage to harp on people's fears of being fat. And the thing is that the overwhelming majority of people in the USA haven't lost a pound since the Pro-Health Laws. Or they've lost it, regained and gained even more.

"So what do they do? They assume that people have to eat even less. And of course the flap about the mortality studies and FatLand citizens living longer made them even angrier. Since FatLand people eat what they want, it undermines the entire case of Big Diet completely. But they keep on going back to weight and diet, as if they were broken records. And we keep publishing things and staging demonstrations.

"We tried to get a permit to demonstrate in front of the courthouse when Sandor was walking in, but they shunted us off to a practically deserted area several blocks away while they let the rabid dieters stand almost next to him. We might try to change that, though." She chuckles. "And don't ask me how, because that's classified. Don't want Big Diet sending its thugs."

"How could they send thugs?" I ask. "Are there any left who are even strong enough?"

"You'd be amazed," Shermaine says. "You have to remember that most people aren't losing weight, just energy. And probably health. But that doesn't matter to Big Diet. We'll keep on fighting as long as we can."

So THEY FIGHT ON, this group of heroic people (the overwhelming majority of FatAndProud's members are women) going against the grain, trying to talk sense in a land where nonsense rules in the form of the Pro-Health Laws. They deserve our admiration and support. But even more than that, they deserve our hopes and prayers.

We in FatLand remember all too well what it was like to live under a cloud, ashamed of ourselves and our bodies, ashamed of trying to measure up to a thin-crazy fatphobic standard of what we were supposed to be and could not possibly be.

One day the USA will toss off the tyranny of the Pro-Health Laws. Until then, we salute our sisters and brothers on the Other Side who wage a neverending battle against injustice of the gravest kind.

The freedoms we FatLanders take for granted are perhaps more fragile than we imagined.

Chapter 14

Joann

As surprised as she was to have been nominated Chair for the Board meeting, Joann tried not to let it show. She did, however, express her appreciation briefly for the Board members' response to what, on the face of it, seemed a rather minor detail, one that might indeed have resulted from a discrepancy.

She said, "I have yet to receive a response from my liaison officer at FatLand National Bank. Reevie now informs me that the Board has also yet to receive a response to their similar and friendly query."

"In that case," Alvin said, "since we are the ones slated to approve any major spending changes by the bank, we are quite justified in demanding an explanation."

"And if none is forthcoming?" Joann said.

"Then we request an appointment with the bank manager and an appointment with their software specialist."

"What's the timeline for this?" Ed asked.

"Four days," Joann said tersely. "They have access to podmail. And now," Joann added, her mouth in a grim line, "Detective Leffler would like to report to us on the progress made in a case that claims our minds and hearts. Detective Leffler."

Leffler stood and inclined his head. "We have received some information we have confirmed possibly links to the crime. Since it concerns FatLanders, I wished to consult with the Board before taking further steps."

"Please tell us the nature of this information," Joann said.

"We isolated the ISP numbers and computer ownership of FatLanders accessing a site that is violently anti-FatLand. We then located comments on the blog that is part of the site. The list of accessors and commenters is as follows." He produced the printout and handed it to Joann.

Joann looked at the list, then gripped the corner of the table. She tried to speak, but couldn't. Ed, who had been sitting next to Joann, stood and peered over her shoulder. On reading the list, he sat down again and clutched his head.

"What's the matter?" Reevie said, standing and running to the podium. She put a hand on Joann's shoulder.

Joann motioned to the list. Reevie read the names to herself, then gasped.

Alvin shot out of his chair. "What the—" He extended a hand. Reevie handed him the list. He read: "The following FatLanders have been active in 'Chewing The Fat,' a violently anti-FatLand blog, for more than two years. They are as follows: Jesse Torelli, Aimee Johnson, Jenna Johnson.'

"My God," he whispered. "Why?"

"That's what we have to find out," Reevie said.

Chapter 15

The Johnsons

REEVIE OBSERVED HER TWO DAUGHTERS as they sat down on the couch in the family room. "Everyone loves them," rang in her ears from a comment made by someone at one of the Board dinners—probably Margaret, she thought. Would Margaret now do them a favor and keep this out of the news? Did she even have a right to ask?

She tried to look at her daughters as if she were seeing them for the first time—Aimee, with that extra rich skin tone and long hair and luminous eyes that could sway a theater, Jenna, with a little more brooding and somber expression, quieter, thoughtfully lovely, with more compact movements. No. There was simply nothing that even an experienced eye would catch that betrayed this monstrous disconnect and chaos.

"Now," she said as Alvin stared at them, not bothering to mask his shame and horror, "please explain to me how you got started in this, and why."

"It was a joke at first," Aimee said, not meeting her eyes. "We thought the whole thing was a joke."

"How did you learn about the site?" Alvin asked, keeping his voice low and harsh.

"Jesse told us."

"How did he learn about it?"

"A friend of his."

"From FatLand?"

"No."

"Really," Alvin said. "Then how did he manage to become friends with this person?"

"Chat room," Jenna said. She looked at the arm of the couch as if it had grown wings or horns.

"What kind of chat room?"

"It's for people who fool around with different kinds of things."

"Like?"

"Bombs. Explosives. Fires."

"Wonderful," Reevie whispered. "Explosives. Were you involved in this, too?"

"No," Aimee said. "That's not our thing."

"Nice to know," Alvin said. "Then how did 'Chewing the Fat' become your thing?"

"Jesse told us about it. He said it was fun to read because the posts were so stupid."

"And that's why you joined?"

Aimee hung her head. "No."

"Then?"

"I liked a friend of Jesse's," Jenna said.

"The one he met in the chat room?"

"No, another one."

"And he was involved in the site?"

"Only in the blog," Jenna said. "He believed in the idea of people's bodies being set free."

"Set free how?"

"He said that bodies were meant to dance and jump and explore and experience joy."

"Then why did he hate FatLand?"

"He said that I was cool, and that he'd like to get to know me better, but that most FatLanders were bitches and dykes."

"Wonderful," Reevie said. "Did you get to know him better?"

"Yes."

"How?"

"We met at The Laurels twice."

"Laurels? That's in Colorado! How did you get out of FatLand?" The words crashed into her mind again: "It's the latest fad. They visit to watch thin people."

"When you were away at Board meetings," Aimee said, "we used to go with Jesse."

"To see this person?"

"Not only to see him," Aimee said. "We wanted to see what it was like, to be out of FatLand. And to see what boys were like on the Other Side. And people."

Chapter 16

The Torellis

DETECTIVE LEFFLER SAT ON A WINGBACK CHAIR in the Torelli home. "I hear you were head of your class in FatLand Tech," he said to Jesse.

Jesse nodded.

"What were your favorite subjects?"

"Oil science, hydrology, physical chemistry."

Joann and Ed had agreed not to be present at the time of the questioning. They sat upstairs in the same room. Joann looked at Ed sitting next to her on the chaise lounge, constructed and upholstered in FatLand per the rules of the territory. "What will happen?" she whispered.

"Life," Ed whispered back. "Mandatory sentence for murder in FatLand." He stared aimlessly at the floor. "How did it happen? I just don't understand. We gave our kids everything."

"We tried," Joann said, and reached for his hand. "You know something, though, Ed? I think Jesse was starting to feel trapped here. I wonder if a lot of our young people are feeling the same way. I mean, FatLand is like heaven on Earth to us because we know what it's like to be persecuted for being fat. But they never knew that. They grew up taking it for granted that it was okay, even normal, to be fat, and that there was nothing they had to apologize for. So this small piece of heaven of ours was just too small for them."

"What I don't understand, though," Ed said, "is why *her*. Why Amiyah? What did she ever do to him? And why now? What was going on there?"

"I think Detective Leffler is going to try to find out exactly those things," Joann said.

When Detective Leffler knocked on their bedroom door, Ed and Joann were fast asleep. He was about to leave when he heard the door open.

"I know it's late," he said, "but I would like both of you to come downstairs. I think we all need to talk with Jesse."

Five minutes later Joann and Ed sat on the sectional not far from but not next to Jesse. Leffler said, "Please tell your parents what you told me."

"I don't know where to start," Jesse said. His long lashes swept onto his cheek as they grazed his dark brown eyes.

"I want you to tell them specifically about what led up to what happened the night the bombing killed Amiyah."

"Okay," Jesse said and turned his head slightly to one side. "It was like this. Dennie Chase, the guy who owned 'Chewing the Fat,' and I became kind of friendly. He asked me to do him this favor. He said he wanted to scare someone in FatLand, but only scare them, nothing else. He said he wanted me to construct a bomb like in a gangster movie. He told me that he wanted it put in a car. When I asked him why, he said that the person had been in his face way too much lately, and he wanted to teach them a lesson. I said, 'Hey man, are you sure they'll be away from the car?' He said, 'Absolutely.' So I planted the bomb in the place he directed. It was in a parking place. It was under Amiyah's rented car."

"You had no idea that it was her car?" Leffler said.

"None," Jesse said.

"It didn't occur to you to ask more about this person supposedly getting in Dennie's face?" Joann said.

"I assumed it was some business competitor," Jesse said.

"So you planted the bomb for him?" Leffler said.

"Yes. As he asked."

"What did you get out of doing this?" Ed asked harshly in a voice very unlike his own.

"Dennie was my friend," Jesse said.

"You don't have friends here?" Joann asked.

"He was also in touch with Mira," Jesse said. "I wanted to make sure that someone was looking out for her."

Joann looked to one side. Tears trickled slowly down Ed's face.

"And you thought no one would find out about any of this?" Detective Leffler said.

"I wasn't sure," Jesse said. "I was thinking of going to the Other Side. To be with Mira."

"Do you have any idea of what will happen to you now?" Detective Leffler said.

"Not really," Jesse said.

"Do you care?" Detective Leffler asked.

"I guess so," Jesse said, looking at his parents in the low light of the night lamp. "I didn't think I would, but I do."

TEN MINUTES LATER Detective Leffler podmailed Detective Vance in Colorado: "Pick up Dennie Chase and hold him for questioning."

Chapter 17

Sandor

SANDOR LOOKED OUT at the audience. Extremely hostile, except for the female reporter from *FatLand News*. Thank God for her. He wondered how she managed to withstand the looks, jeers and catcalls he knew she would receive on her way to the courthouse.

"Please stand to receive the verdict and sentence," the judge, a woman, intoned. Sandor noted that she wore a navy dress without any curves or markings, as did most professional female Other Siders. The male professionals wore navy suits. *Looks like a uniform,* he thought.

"Jury members," she said, "what is your verdict in the case of *Stark vs. Forman?*"

"We find the defendant guilty," the foreman, a securities analyst, said.

"I shall now pronounce sentence," the judge announced. "Sandor Forman, you have been found guilty of reneging on your contract with Complete Fitness. The maximum sentence for such an offense carries a jail term of four years. And that is what this court sentences. To start tomorrow. This time." She banged the gavel.

"What?" Ava was on her feet. "This is a first offense and the defendant in such cases is usually sentenced to pay a fine. How can you even justify any of this?"

"You will be held in contempt of court if you continue to heckle," the judge warned.

"Your sentence will held in contempt in every newspaper in Fat-Land," Ava responded.

"If I'm supposed to be shaking in my shoes, I'm not," the judge said. She turned on her heels and left the courtroom, followed by the sergeant-at-arms.

"You will be," Ava said. She looked at Sandor. He looked back, still in shock.

Ava crossed over to where he stood alone as Coloradoans looked at them both. "How about dinner tonight?" she said. "At The Laurels. It's on the *News.*"

Sandor grinned. "That'll tide me over for the next four years."

"You're not going to serve four years," Ava said. "And definitely not in Colorado."

"ARE YOU READY?" Ava asked as Sandor finished the last spoonful of rice pudding with whipped cream.

"Ready to go to jail?"

"Ready to leave."

"I suppose so. Can I stretch my legs a little first?"

"Sure," Ava said.

"I mean," Sandor said, "who knows when I'll get the chance next? I assume their prisons allow exercise, but it's probably in one of those yards you used to see on video."

Ava walked with him to the end of the parking lot. As they walked back, Sandor stiffened. "What's that?" he asked as he saw three women coming toward him.

"Sorry we had to do it this way," Ava said, "but it's for your own good."

One of the women pushed something into Sandor's arm. He went limp. "He's out," Patty said. "Let's get him into the van."

The women lifted Sandor into the van and wrapped him in blankets. "At least he won't be cold when he wakes up," Crystal said.

"Leave him room for breathing," Shermaine said.

"You know that you can't return," Ava told them.

"We know," Patty said.

"Ready?" Shermaine asked.

"Ready," Crystal said.

"Ready," Ava said.

Shermaine started the van. They cruised on the moonlit, mostly empty highway.

"Is it fixed with the checkpoint on the FatLand side?" Crystal asked.

"Yep," Ava said. "Margaret was on audio with them a little while ago. They're ready."

"What if the Colorado side starts shooting?" Patty said.

"We gun the pedal and pray," Shermaine said.

"How's he doing back there?" Ava asked a few minutes later.

"Sleeping like a baby," Patty assured her. "He'll be fine."

The last exit before FatLand loomed up.

"We ready?" Shermaine said.

"Yes," the rest of the women responded.

"Slow and polite," Ava said. "Let's see what they say first."

THEY REACHED THE RAMP for the checkpoint on the Colorado side. Shermaine stopped the car. "We all know what to do," she said. "Crystal, you have that pie ready and warm?"

"Heated on the portable. It's ready to go. Making me hungry."

Shermaine laughed. "Yeah, it even reaches up here. Patty, you have the papers?"

"Right here."

"Okay." She resumed driving. The traffic was nonexistent on the ramp at 4 a.m. "Looks like we'll be the only ones at the checkpoint."

As instructed by the sign, they stopped the car at the booth.

"Papers," the guard said tersely.

Patty handed the papers to the guard. They contained the passports of all present, including Sandor.

"What's with him?" the guard pointed to Sandor. "Sleeping it off?"

"Yes," Shermaine said.

"I'll have a look around, if you don't mind."

Crystal produced the pie. "We're taking a couple of these back with us."

The guard said, "By your laws, it is allowed." He was clearly not happy with that fact. He gazed at Sandor again. "You sure he's sleeping?"

"Positive," Crystal affirmed. The guard looked at the pie. Following his mournful gaze, Crystal said, "Listen, we don't need both of these. Why don't you accept this one, with our compliments?"

"Really?" The guard beamed. "You sure?"

"Absolutely," Shermaine affirmed.

The guard turned his eyes on Ava. "Haven't I seen you somewhere before?"

"On the way in, I think," Ava said politely.

"Oh, yeah." The guard looked at her indifferently, then turned his eyes back to the pie. "Apple?" he said, his breath coming more quickly.

"Dutch apple with raisins," Patty said.

"Oh, God." He took the pie in his hands, inhaled, sighed. "Ladies, you've just made my night. Have a safe trip home."

None of them dared to breathe until they passed the sign that said, "You are now entering FatLand."

Part III

Chapter 1

Ava

FatLand Free News
March 28

CHASE CONFESSES
LINK TO STARK FOUND
FORMAN NOT FOUND
BY AVA BRYER

IT WAS DRIZZLING AND CHILLY when Detective Carl Vance confronted the young man and said, "Mr. Chase, you're under arrest for murder."

"I will answer no questions until I am in the presence of a lawyer," Dennis Chase answered.

The next day two detectives interrogated Chase. What they found amazed them.

Chase started his website, "Chewing the Fat," at the instigation of Winston Stark. Chase stated also that its goal was not only to demoralize FatLanders, but to convince Coloradoans to join Complete Fitness.

The trouble started, Chase said, when Amiyah, the beautiful, curvaceous, irresistible Egyptian dancer, appeared in commercials for GymNotTrim. Suddenly Coloradoans, and many in other states as well, started to desert Complete Fitness and join GymNotTrim in record numbers.

"He was scared," Chase said. "Well, not scared. Angry. And then he said, 'Will no one rid me of this Egyptian succubus?'"

"So," Chase continued, "I thought he wanted Amiyah out of there. But I told him that was simply not right. I said, 'How about if we just scare her? You know, plant something near her car but not near enough to hurt her physically?'"

"He said that would be okay. So I arranged for the device to be planted. It was supposed to be near her car. But somehow she didn't park in the usual place. She parked right over the device. It was horrible. We really didn't mean for it to happen."

Intent aside, Mr.Winston Stark is now being questioned by the Colorado State police. He will be questioned in turn by Fat-Land detectives.

Many FatLanders feel a certain amount of vindication in the wake of Mr. Stark's continuing vendetta against GymNotTrim, which led to the trial of CEO Sandor Forman in Colorado. As of today, Mr. Forman, who disappeared the night after being sentenced to four years in a Colorado prison, has not been found.

"I KEPT JESSE AND AIMEE AND JENNA out of there," Ava told Margaret. "I guess Jesse will be sentenced today."

"Tonight," Margaret said. "You coming?"

"Yes," Ava said.

"Still bitter?"

"Yes," she said. "Not quite as much, though. It doesn't help anything."

Chapter 2

Sandor

DARA WATCHED AS SANDOR opened his eyes. She continued to watch as he closed them, opened them again, and closed them one more time. Then he opened them wide.

"Oh, God," he said. "They put something in the prison food. Whatever they call food, anyway. I'm hallucinating, I guess. Someone get me out of this."

"You're not hallucinating," Dara said. "And you're not anywhere near any prison."

He gazed at her. "Well, I trust you, babe. I always did. So I guess I'm not in prison, anyway."

"No, you're not," Dara said, closing her eyes to get rid of unshed tears and smiling wide.

"So where the hell am I?"

"I personally think it's closer to heaven," Dara said. "But heaven on Earth. You're very much healthy and alive. You are in one of FatLand's safe houses in Fabrey Woods."

"Oh wow," Sandor said, sitting up. "Hey, did you put these pajamas on me? They're great. What happened? How did I get here?"

As Dara told him the story of the midnight kidnapping and ride, complete with pie, Sandor started to laugh. "Those FatAndProud chicks are amazing," he said. "But not more amazing than you. So you managed the whole thing."

"I had lots of help," she said. "Ava did a lot. So did everyone in FatAndProud. So did Margaret."

"Margaret Clancy of *FatLand Free News?* Good lord. She used to hate me."

"She didn't," Dara said. "And I think she's a fan of yours now."

"So how many people know I'm here?"

"Just a few." Shermaine walked into the room. "You're looking great. I was worried about the side effects, but I see now that nothing happened."

Sandor put out a hand. "Anything is better than the bars of an Other Side prison," he said. "Thank you for saving me."

"You're very welcome." Shermaine took his hand and shook it.

"So how does this work?" Sandor asked. "This safe house."

"We stay until the ruckus dies down," Shermaine said.

Sandor grinned. "We?"

"You and me and Patty and Crystal."

"Sounds like fun," Sandor said, winking at Dara. She pretended to look annoyed, but couldn't hold the expression long enough and started to laugh. "Four of us, eh," Sandor mused. "I know you can't go back. And I don't think you would even want to."

"I had some conflicts about that," Shermaine said. "And so did Patty and Crystal. But you know something? There are plenty of FatAnd-Prouders left to carry on. And they know we couldn't go back."

"Couldn't go back and shouldn't go back," Dara said. "You are heroes to us now, and we want to keep you safe."

Shermaine smiled. "Never been a hero before. Don't know how that goes."

"You stay here," Dara said. "You enjoy life. There are guards who will keep you safe. They have to escort you any place you go. That's the one drawback. But you will find they'll be in awe of you. They'll probably run to get you coffee and anything else you ask."

"I have to explore," Sandor announced. "Oh." He looked at his pajamas. "Clothes would be useful."

"I'll leave you two alone." Shermaine winked at Dara. "But come down for the breakfast buffet. It's awesome."

When Shermaine closed the door, Sandor held out his arms. Dara sat down on the bed and hugged him to her tightly.

"Don't let go," he said.

"I don't intend to," she said.

Chapter 3

The Torellis & Johnsons

THE JUDGE ENTERED. "All rise," the sergeant-at-arms intoned.

The Board members and Jesse rose. Aimee and Jenna rose. The judge sat.

"Under these very unusual circumstances I am called to pronounce sentence on three FatLanders," the judge announced. "The details of the case are as follows. Jesse Torelli, aided and abetted at times by Aimee and Jenna Johnson, did conspire to create and set a device that resulted in the death of an innocent dancer, Amiyah.

"The sentence decreed by law for such an action is life imprisonment for murder in the second degree, with lesser sentences for any who complied or conspired or aided in this action. However, since these are unusual circumstances, they call for an unusual approach. I hereby pronounce sentence as follows.

"Jesse Torelli, you are hereby sentenced to live for fifteen years outside FatLand."

Joann and Ed Torelli gasped and turned their heads away from the judge.

"I am certain," the judge continued, "that this will give you ample time to reflect on your crime. It will also make you understand the gravity of your own actions and what it means to abuse the freedoms given you in this sovereign State. It is also a fitting punishment for one who has proclaimed that he despises FatLand. Live outside for fifteen years and see what it is like. A condition of this sentence is that you cannot be aided by your parents, and that they may not see you until the sentence is completed."

Joann wiped her eyes. "We thank you, your honor," she said.

The judge nodded, then said, "Aimee and Jenna Johnson, I sentence you to live five years outside FatLand. I believe that you were not aware of all of the implications of your actions. Even fools cannot escape punishment if their actions lead to an innocent person's death, even directly. You are not fools, but it is time for you to learn some wisdom. You will be able to see your parents twice a year."

Aimee and Jenna started to cry. Alvin put a handkerchief to his eyes. Reevie sat stonefaced. Ava whispered to her, "It'll be over before you know it. And perhaps it's for the best. Who knows what trouble they could have gotten into."

Reevie didn't reply.

Margaret nodded to the judge and said, "I would like to make a statement on behalf of the Board, Your Honor."

The judge inclined her head. "Proceed."

"Although the actions of the three young people here were at times heinous and often foolish, we the Board understand that two factors were at work. First, that self-hatred was able to enter into the minds of these young people, three of our finest, even though we did our best to shelter them from the kind of hatred we knew on the Other Side when we were young. Second, that they felt hemmed in, somehow trapped, in what may have appeared to them—partly as a result of this self-hatred, but also as a result of their need for exploration as questioning young people—as a place which, instead of being a refuge, had become a prison.

"As a result of these occurrences and circumstances, we the Board of FatLand have initiated the first FatLand Student Exchange Program on the high school and college levels. If anything good is to come out of this sad chain of events, let it be that our thoughtful and questioning young people have a way to see the Other Side firsthand without having to sneak into its borders—a way that is supervised so they will be able to experience life on the Other Side but without its more horrific aspects, and for a comparatively short time. This way they will be able to compare FatLand to the Other Side and will be able to choose freely whether they wish to return or to remain on the Other Side for a longer time. And they will be able to choose freely."

Jesse, Aimee and Jenna looked at Margaret as if they had just been handed a torch in a very dark cave.

Jenna said, "Your Honor, I would like to request permission to address the court and Board, if I may."

"Permission granted."

"What Ms. Clancy has said here tonight is true in every sense. The three of us, FatLanders born and bred, took the privileges of belonging to FatLand very lightly. We started to feel that we were hemmed in, that there was somehow more to life than we had here. We went so far as to commit some very thoughtless actions that resulted in the loss of life of an innocent person. There is no justification for such actions. But we would like all of you to understand that from the time we were young, whenever we questioned our parents or any of you about life on the Other Side, we were simply told that it was a horrible place, and that we were extremely lucky to be here.

"Young people question such simple categorizations. If they are forbidden from exploring something, they will find a way to explore it anyway. In this case, our explorations came at a terrible price. We will have to live with the sadness and shame and knowledge of our actions all our lives. But it is a relief to know that even out of our anger and disgust with our lives here, something good has been created, and perhaps the next generation of FatLanders will be able to question and explore without being fobbed off with simplistic reprimands to value what is in FatLand and not question what is on the Other Side.

"We thank the Board and the court for their understanding. We accept our sentences."

There was no applause, but the Board looked at Jenna as she seated herself again. Reevie looked up for the first time that night.

The judge said, "I am glad the three of you will have a chance to gain understanding of your crimes and of your own lives, and glad that a way has been found to address some of the issues that led to your actions. This session of the court and the Board is now adjourned."

"All rise," the sergeant-at-arms barked.

As Jesse, Aimee and Jenna were led away Reevie wept at last, followed by Alvin, Ed, and—to her own surprise—Margaret.

Ava remained calm outwardly. "It won't bring back Amiyah," she whispered to Margaret, "but it does focus on what caused—what happened to her."

"Does that bring you peace?" Margaret whispered back, her tears stopping.

"Some."

"The next item on the agenda," Joann announced with all the calm she could muster, "is the question of the funds for intra-state spending that seemingly disappeared from the FatLand budget.

"We requested an audience with the person who was in charge of keeping track of these funds, only to learn that she had been transferred. We then requested an audience with the CEO of FatLand National Bank, only to be told that he was busy for the next week. We indicated our displeasure at his answer, and our intent to hire an auditor on our own. Our statement was met by silence.

"It is only today that we learned that the CEO, who was also on our Board, has disappeared. To all intents and purposes he has left FatLand. This of course would be a scandal of major proportions if we did not have a capable, responsible, caring person to assume the executive office and role. But we do have such a person. I am honored to introduce to you Alice Bidewell Adams, formerly Vice Chair of the Board of the FatLand National Bank, now CEO. Welcome, Alice."

"Thanks so much for inviting me," Chair Adams said. "Members of the Board, I am here to report on the omission ably noticed by your present chair, and to offer an explanation of this omission. Within two hours of assuming my new office, I held a meeting of our staff and told them that my highest priority was getting to the bottom of this discrepancy. They immediately started to work on solving the problem.

"It turns out that the capital that normally would have gone to intra-state expenditures and investments was siphoned off by someone in the Bank. I regret to say that it was none other than the former CEO, Drew Harris."

"Yes," Reevie said. "But why did he do it?"

"At this time I would like to present someone with whom you are all familiar as the result of his work on another, related case," Ms. Adams said. "Detective Vance."

Detective Vance, who had been sitting on a side-chair, stood up. "We confronted Winston Stark yesterday about the Amiyah case," he said.

"What we learned bears directly on the discrepancy you noticed.

"It turns out that Drew Harris siphoned off the funds from your intra-state budget to finance the building and explosion of the device, as well as the planning of the crime. At least some of you here may be aware that Harris and Stark were close friends. Dennie Chase was exaggerating his importance and his role in the case, it turns out. His job was to get someone to make and plant the device in FatLand. It was Harris's job to secure the funding."

"But that was quite a sizable amount," Ed pointed out. "Jesse didn't see any of it. How could they justify siphoning such an amount for one operation?"

"It was also used for Harris's escape," Vance said.

"Was it supposed to be used for Jesse's escape, as well?" Ed asked.

"Not that we can see."

"So this amount was also supposed to finance Harris's removal to and residence in Colorado?"

"That is correct."

"He was on the Board," Joann said. "He knew all of us."

"I think that was Stark's plan."

"You mean that Harris was in effect a spy?" Margaret asked.

"Yes."

"That does explain a lot," Margaret said. "The papers Stark owns always seemed to be aware of news from FatLand as quickly as we were, or even more quickly. I always wondered how they did it. Now I know."

Detective Vance nodded. "Are there any more questions?" he asked.

The Board was quiet. "Thank you so much for sharing your knowledge with us," Joann said.

"I would like a word with you before you leave," Vance said. Joann nodded.

As the members of the Board filed out, Joann caught Ed's eyes. He mouthed, "I'll be in the car."

Vance fiddled with his Pod. "Ms. Torelli," he said, "a word of advice. I think that if you offered to drop charges against Stark for the murder, he would drop charges against Forman."

"The two are not comparable in our minds," Joann said with some heat.

"I realize that," Detective Vance agreed. "But three of your kids are going to be staying outside FatLand for extended periods of time. You wouldn't want anything to happen to them, would you?"

"Dear God," Joann said. "Is this blackmail?"

"Consider it a word to the wise. And you know, people can only remain in safe houses for so long. They have to come out eventually."

"So," Joann said, "that bloody spy Harris. But I compliment you on your intelligence gathering."

"No spies, Ms. Torelli. Just wisdom gained over the years."

"For my part," Joann said, "the answer would be a resounding 'No.' But I am obliged to put your offer to the Board. I will call another meeting at the earliest possible time."

"A wise decision," Vance said.

What You Need to Know about Living in FatLand

FatLand PRIDES ITSELF on being self-sufficient, on providing whatever goods and services are necessary and/or requested by its citizens. Thus no exports of any kind are allowed, although we have developed some of our industries and services so highly that they are eagerly sought after in different locations around the globe. In this way FatLand always runs a surplus and is also able to keep its tax burden comparatively light for its citizens.

For this reason, FatLand's customs officers are very carefully trained and highly paid. Packages containing gifts are checked to make sure that no hazardous goods or commercial imports get through the FatLand checkpoint. Any hazardous goods are either imploded or sent back to their countries of origin. Any commercial imports are sent back to their points of origin, and the addressees are questioned.

FatLand officers are also quite careful about checking the credentials of those who seek to enter FatLand. Anyone who wishes to visit FatLand must submit our visa form six months in advance, with travel plans carefully detailed and photostats of transportation tickets. Anyone who wishes to gain FatLand residence must be a relative of a citizen or willing to undergo our test of intent twice a year. Immigrants who have not yet had their status adjusted must report to FatLand Customs and Immigration Officers twice a year. Immigrants who have been granted Permanent Resident status must report to our Customs and Immigration Officers once a year.

The most serious complaint that can be lodged against anyone in FatLand, whether a visitor, aspiring resident, or citizen, is that of anti-fat or non-accepting behavior. If such a complaint is lodged, it is investigated with exceeding thoroughness. In the case of judgment against the defendant, one appeal is permitted. If that appeal is lost, the defendant is deported immediately. However, if the complaint is found to be spurious, the same punishment, that of exile, is meted out to the plaintiff.

FatLand celebrates its Founding Days from May 1 to May 10 of every year. The highlight of the celebration includes a gala festival for No-Diet Day on May 6. Food, games, prizes, readings and concerts commemorate the bravery and foresight of the Founders of FatLand, and its present unique and tolerant sovereignty as a haven for Size Acceptance.

Chapter 4

Shermaine

THESE DAYS I SAY "good morning" and really mean it, as in the old Mamas and Papas song.

I cannot get used to living without the burden of expecting hate-filled glances and venom whispered just this side of audibility. No, actually, I can get used to it. Most of the time I just have trouble believing it.

I had prepared myself to live a life of struggle on the Other Side, as people here call it, somehow finding the resources inside myself to keep reassuring others that it was fine to be fat, even and especially when we were not allowed to buy most snacks if we were over a certain weight. Even during the weekly weigh-ins.

If you were lucky you got to be weighed more or less in private. If not, you were out there, with people staring bugeyed as the scale pushed beyond 300 and you had to justify to some vicious young toughs why you continued to weigh more than 300 even under strict eating requirements. They always thought we were stealing food. (Never mind that everyone in Colorado knew about The Laurels and tried to get there at least once every two months to eat "real" food. Never mind that most people, when surveyed by a woman's mag, said that they would rather have good food again than sex.)

Even now, a week after having arrived here, I have trouble asking for what I want, and trouble not looking over my shoulder when I eat to see if the Pro-Health Enforcers are coming. When I told this to Dara, she actually cried. Then she said, "What you say upsets me terribly, but it also reassures me that we did the right thing. I am so glad you're here, and that Sandor is here, instead of being—here."

"I'm glad, too," I told her.

Glad? I still cannot believe it. The whole thing reminds me of *The Little Princess*, which I read when I was little. The "princess" goes from little rich girl to very very poor to cared-for and loved again when her father's partner finally locates her and takes her from the wretched school whose headmistress tried to overwork and starve her.

On the most material, gut level, I have to keep reminding myself that reaching for or asking for a piece of bread with butter (and the FatLand butter is superb!) is now as natural as waking up in the morning. I won't start on how it felt to sleep peacefully at last, in this Safe House in the woods. It was difficult for me even to get six good hours on the Other Side in all the years since the Pro-Health Laws were passed.

I now wonder if certain racist tendencies were reinforced by the Pro-Health Laws, as well—were black women of size being stigmatized again, as we were in the years when people called us "welfare queens"? It sure felt that way at times. Here, when I do emerge from the Safe House to go shopping, people smile and nod and say hello. It makes me want to sob, because I had forgotten what it was like to have people smile and accept me for what I am in my own skin.

I feel as if my body and mind and heart are singing. Ironically, I might have lost a few pounds. Don't know why, but I have to get the next size down these days. In all the years under the Pro-Health Laws, I did not lose one ounce.

I become sad again when I think of my FatAndProud sisters still on the Other Side, but even sadder when I think of my blood sisters and their kids. Those kids will never know what it is to grow up in a place where they don't have to worry night and day about their size and what they eat. Besides everything else, the Pro-Health Laws just about ended childhood. (And the number of violent shows kids watched skyrocketed.) How can you play happily when you are preoccupied with eating the "right" things and worrying about the Enforcers if they happen to catch you with an ice cream cone?

"Sonny, where did you get that cone?"

"My mom got it on the ration coupon. Would you like to see?"

"We'll have a look at that, if you don't mind."

Sounds like war, doesn't it? And yet the real war is between the megacorporations behind the Pro-Health Laws and the rest of us. Has nothing to do with nationalities or religions or territories or the usual stuff. Has everything to do with a few people thinking they can and should tell other people what to do and how to live their lives.

But wait, isn't that what causes war? Maybe eating or not eating has become a religion of its own on the Other Side. And the people who rammed the Pro-Health Laws through are the high priests.

Well, I have news for them. Their days are numbered. Remember that old Sixties song, "Whatcha gonna do about me?" I keep thinking of the line about how when they shoot us down, more join. I keep thinking of the people in prison on the Other Side because they violated the Pro-Health Laws. I keep dreaming that they all somehow manage to escape and get to FatLand, just as I dream about my sisters' kids.

The one down side—we are allowed these podmails, but no voice mail or conversations. They want to make sure we're safe. According to my visitors, there are people on the Other Side who want to bump us off simply for managing to get away, let alone kidnapping Sandor. But in my heart of hearts, I think they simply can't stand the thought of us as "fat and happy" once more.

Speaking of which, Sandor is here now. He wants the four of us and Dara to go for a picnic on the north side of the house, where there are new spring flowers. Our security detail will of course be present. But it sounds almost too pleasant to be real.

Part of me keeps reassuring itself that nothing bad will happen. The other part of me will keep looking for the Enforcers to swoop down on us and drag us back. And I'd bet anything that Patty and Crystal feel exactly the same way.

We are still not used to living with happiness or allowing ourselves to deserve it.

Chapter 5

Mira

MIRA REGARDED THE FACES around her. Some seemed kind and encouraging; the rest seemed skeptical.

"Please state your name," the woman sitting in the middle of the rug said.

"My name is Mira Torelli."

"Mira, please tell us why you wish to join FatAndProud."

"When I came here from FatLand," Mira said, "I was thrilled to be accepted as I was and for what I was. I thought I was really free at last. I didn't know that I, a thin person, would be watched and monitored as carefully as the fat people here. As the months passed, I started to realize that in FatLand, people really do live free free of monitoring, free of worry about whatever their weights are and whatever their body shapes are.

"I think it is both wrong and horrible that people here, in Colorado and the rest of the United States, are forced to live their lives under the Pro-Health Laws and constant anxiety about what they eat and weigh. No one has the right to tell anyone else what to eat and what to weigh. My parents are both fat, and they are happy exactly as they are. Sometimes they get exercise, and sometimes they don't.

"My brother Jesse—" here she gulped as she tried—and managed— not to cry, "was misled by someone who told him FatLand is a dinky little place with no charm and sophistication. I see now that instead of FatLand aiming to be like the Other Side, the Other Side should aim to be like FatLand.

"And when I saw clips of the way people were treated in prisons here for disobeying and rebelling against the Pro-Health Laws, I knew my place was here, with FatAndProud, even though I am not fat myself. I have had to learn the hard way that appearances of all kinds can deceive."

"Mira, we are now going to interview you more thoroughly." The leader beckoned to another woman, who said, "We would like to know why you left FatLand in the first place."

"I left because I felt that as a thin person, I was considered unattractive."

"And you felt you would be considered attractive here?"

"Yes."

"Do you feel that this has happened?"

"To an extent," Mira said, "but it doesn't make up for the lack of freedom I or any of us experience here."

"Would you go back to FatLand if you could?" another member asked.

"That is a difficult question," Mira admitted. "Sometimes I would like to go back. I miss my parents and my brother very much. But I now think that my place is here in Colorado, helping people to disobey the Pro-Health Laws."

"What if you had to go to prison as an accomplice of someone who disobeyed the Pro-Health Laws?"

"I would go."

The room broke into spontaneous applause. The leader said, "Mira, I too am pleased with your answers. But be aware that we are coming to the time when you may indeed be asked to do exactly what you have said."

"I am aware of that," Mira said. She looked around the room. "I think a few of you here may be aware that there is another reason I wish to give my time and life to FataAdProud. I feel that even though I did not know and did not choose to be, I may have been one of the factors in the killing of Amiyah, the Egyptian dancer who appeared in advertisements for GymNotTrim. I feel the least I can do to set things right and to honor her is to work with FatAndProud."

The members lowered their eyes. The leader said, "Mira Torelli, do you swear on all you hold dear to be loyal to the objectives of FatAndProud and to value the lives of your sister and fellow members as you do your own?"

"I do," Mira said.

"Please raise your right hand and repeat the following words: I, Mira Torelli, vow that I will work untiringly for the liberation of fat people throughout the United States of America and will not cease in my efforts until the Pro-Health Laws and any other laws like them have been nullified and voided."

Mira repeated the words.

"You are now an honorary member of FatAndProud," the leader said. "Congratulations."

The other members applauded. "Welcome," one said.

"Coffee and cake upstairs," the leader said, grinning. "Sarma and Aloise, you stand guard. Signal if you see anyone unauthorized approaching."

"Will do." The two women left to take up posts in the front and back of the house respectively.

"Do you always have guards at meetings?" Mira asked as she followed the others upstairs.

"Always," the leader said. "By the way, call me Carol."

"Thanks, Carol," Mira said.

"As a matter of fact," Carol said, "your first assignment will be learning how to be a guard."

Chapter 6

The Safe House

"I WANT PLAIN OLD HARDBOILED EGGS with mayonnaise," Patty said, grinning.

"I want gooey peanut butter with jelly," Crystal said, beaming.

"I want buffalo wings with celery and ranch dressing," Shermaine said, winking.

Louanne, the cook said, "Come on. That isn't a picnic, that's a snack."

Sandor, who had just come downstairs, said, "Okay, how about this? Steak tips and asparagus tips alfredo with the right noodles."

All of them nodded appreciatively. "Now you're talking," Louanne said.

"What about you, babe?" Sandor said to Dara, who was looking around the villa-sized kitchen in approval.

"Anything with chocolate or cheese. Or both."

"I have been inspired," Louanne said. She started assembling ingredients and said to the undercook, Mikey, "Do the steak at the last minute and get the asparagus ready." She pointed at the women looking on. "Here, be useful." She brought out peanut butter, three kinds of jelly, and two enriched breads.

Crystal said, "Oh, wow," and opened the breads. The other women started to open the peanut butter and jelly.

"Put up the hardboiled eggs now, too," Louanne said to Mikey. "And for you, sweetie," she said to Dara, "we'll do some chocolate chip cheesecake bars."

"I would swoon," Crystal said, "but I am too busy and happy."

145

Sandor said, "I'll alert the security people."

"Oh, why?" Patty sighed. "It feels kinda funny to have to tell them every time."

"Sandor is one hundred percent right," Shermaine said.

THREE HOURS LATER, the four women helped Louanne and Mikey assemble the picnic basket.

"I threw in some Valencia oranges," Louanne said. "They grow so nicely in our hothouses this time of year. There's cold white wine and some Fuji apple juice, and some pear nectar and raspberry soda. Thermos of hot tea with lemon and one with hot mocha."

Patty sighed in pleasure.

"Do you want to walk," Shermaine asked, "or should the security people drive us?"

"Let's walk," Crystal said. "I missed walking so much in Colorado. I used to love to walk, but then after the Pro-Health Laws, people used to make such nasty remarks. A few of them even threw things."

"THIS IS INCREDIBLE," Patty said as they wended their way up and down a gentle hill on one of the trails. "I feel as if I can breathe again. All of me."

"I feel like singing," Crystal said. Instead, she skipped a little, then danced.

Dara held hands unabashedly with Sandor, who seemed peacefully bemused and picked a few wildflowers, which he then tucked behind her ears.

The security detail followed with the baskets on motorcycles.

"Let's put the blankets here," Shermaine said as they came to a small clearing. The sun shone in the clearing, but aspen and larch trees shaded the upland side.

They spread the blankets. The security detail stopped and unpacked and spread the picnic baskets. Since there was more than the five of them could eat in several meals, they offered some of each course to the five security staff, who accepted and stood not far from the blankets as they munched.

"Oh, God," Crystal said, "I wish Angelina and Corey could be here with us. I feel guilty that we left them there and now—"

"But we took a risk," Shermaine reminded her. "We could have ended up in prison. Remember?"

"Yeah," Crystal agreed.

"And you saved me," Sandor said. "And I thank you ten thousand times each day in my thoughts. I was the one who was supposed to be in prison. But thanks to you, I'm not."

"Oh, eat your steak and asparagus alfredo," Shermaine said impatiently, still embarrassed when Sandor thanked them. "Only a man could come up with such an improbable dish."

"Improbable but good," Patty said.

"Amen to that," Crystal agreed.

THEY WERE STARTING TO SAMPLE the chocolate chip cheesecake bars, which they all agreed were proof that they were in heaven and not on Earth anymore, when Dara stood up suddenly. "Do you hear that?" she said.

"Hear what?"

The noise became louder.

"Sounds like a helicopter," Sandor said. "That's strange. There's no traffic here."

The security detail, on their feet once more, approached Dara. "Ma'am," they said, "we think it would be best if you all went back to the house now. We've ordered a vehicle. Until then, we want you all to lie down. We're going to cover you with a few camouflage blankets."

Without a word, they all lay down in the grass. The security detail covered everyone. Five minutes later, the droning of the helicopter grew fainter, then faded altogether.

The van arrived. The five entered it quietly.

"OVER SO SOON?" Louanne asked as they came back into the house. "Didn't like the food?"

"We loved it," Dara said, "but someone or something didn't like that we loved it."

"The security people thought we'd better return," Sandor added. "They said that until further notice, it would be safer for us to stay in the house."

Trying not to show her anxiety and disappointment, Shermaine said, "Anyone up for Pod scrabble?"

"You can't beat me," Dara said.

"Oh, no?"

"I think I need a nap," Patty said. "Or something."

"They'll keep it out of the news, won't they?" Crystal asked.

"That's a good question," Sandor said. "I'm going to check with a few people now."

Chapter 7

Margaret & Ava

"I'm not printing it, and that's that." Margaret said.

"Then," Ava said, "you're going against your own code of journalistic ethics, and you're being completely unfair to all FatLanders. Come on, Marge, they damned well deserve to know when Other Side helicopters barge into their airspace for spying purposes."

"But that is precisely my point," Margaret said. "We simply do not know if the helicopter was here for spying purposes or just strayed off course. Until we know for certain, we would be doing FatLanders a disservice to harp on it and scare them. Especially the people in the Safe House. You know what they went through because you helped them save Sandor. Do you want us to be the ones who compromise their safety?"

"I think it's more unsafe for FatLanders not to know. This way, if any of them saw more helicopters, they would be prepared. Do you want to let the people in the Safe House think that this is a burden they have to carry all by themselves?"

"The last thing I want is for other FatLanders to complain that the people in the Safe House may be endangering the safety of others. Which they are not, in my opinion."

"That's a straw man argument," Ava said. "How can they complain if they don't know that there are people in the Safe House? And how can they draw any conclusions regarding the helicopter and the people in the Safe House if they don't know where the helicopter was coming from or where it was headed?"

"If they don't know there are people in the Safe House, don't you think we want to keep the fact of there being people in the Safe House among as few people as possible for the longest time?"

"But that just makes my case stronger," Ava said. "If they don't know that there are people in the Safe House, but they do see more helicopters, at least we will know about it soon enough to make sure that the people in the Safe House stay safe."

"Just one thing," Margaret said. "What if other FatLanders see perfectly legal FatLand traffic helicopters, or small planes, or Other Side helicopters, or international small planes, and start getting panicked? Do you really want to start the War of the Worlds again over imaginary threats?"

Ava sighed. "I don't want to start anything," she said. "I just feel Fat-Landers are entitled to know about possible threats so they can protect themselves."

"But until we know exactly what that helicopter was doing here, why it was here, where it was from, and how it got here, we cannot possibly classify it as a threat."

"Compromise," Ava said. "If we get the five W's and the 'H,' will you print it then?"

"I will consider printing it," Margaret said. "But I won't bind or commit myself to printing it."

Chapter 8

The FatLand Board

"WE ARE GATHERED HERE tonight," Margaret said, "to make decisions that will influence the next fifteen years of FatLand history.

"Detective Vance from the Other Side has sent us an offer made by Winston Stark. He offers to drop charges against Sandor for reneging on his contract with Complete Fitness if we drop charges against him, Dennie Chase, and Drew Harris for the murder of Amiyah.

"I would like to say a few words before we go into debate on this topic. I will say them because unlike the great majority of FatLand Board meetings, this is a closed meeting in which only Board members are allowed to be present.

"All of us here know that the safety and welfare of the four people in the Safe House, including Sandor, who is here tonight, will be directly affected by what we conclude and decide. I would also like to note that those four people are the ones who would most want us to make the decision that we feel would benefit FatLand the most. They are the ones who risked their lives for FatLanders. They would not be happy if we sold their heroism short by making whatever appeared to be the easiest decision.

"With this, I would like to call on Ed Torelli to begin debate."

Ed stood. He wore his usual flannel shirt. Joann had long despaired of getting him to change into anything resembling a suit. But by now FatLanders were so used to seeing him in his trademark flannel shirt that they would have been surprised and unsettled to see him in anything else. And as Ed pointed out to everyone, FatLand textile concerns made excellent flannel shirts.

"It's like this," he began. "My two girls made what turned out to be a few mistakes in association. But they were serious mistakes. I thought their judgment was sounder than that. They were all based on the ignorance of youth. But they were also made because Aimee and Jenna didn't know anything about the world outside. Thus they were willing to swallow a lot of lies about the place they themselves lived in and about the place we all left more than twenty years ago.

"I want Sandor here not to have to travel with a security detail every time he goes outside. I want him and the other people in the Safe House to be able not to worry about Other Side helicopters trailing them or even kidnapping them back. But if we say that his so-called crime is equal to that committed by Winston Stark, then we make Stark's crime sound a lot less serious than it is. And we end up calling Sandor's sound judgment a crime, which it damn well was not. That also includes what they call a crime, which was in kidnapping him from Colorado. But since FatLand has no extradition treaty with Colorado or with the USA, we are not even bound to deliver Sandor or the folks in the Safe House to them anyway.

"To my mind, what is going on on the Other Side is the real crime: starving folks for no good reason or just because they happen to weigh more than some fat-phobic health professional thinks they should weigh. We even have the mortality stats on our side, after three studies. But you know what? Even if we didn't, it still wouldn't matter. No one has a right to starve anyone, whatever they weigh.

"But I think that if we allow Stark to get out of his real crime, he will think he can get away with anything he decides to do against Fat-Land.

"So I would vote not to accept Detective Vance's offer. If we have to protect Sandor and the people in the Safe House more carefully, we can do it and we will do it."

Alvin, whose brows rose slightly when Ed mentioned "the girls," opened his mouth, but a look from Reevie shut it. When Ed had finished he said to Margaret, "May I speak next?"

Margaret nodded. "The chair recognizes Alvin Johnston."

"First of all," he began, "I agree with everything my friend and colleague Ed Torelli has said. The most unfortunate associations led Jesse and our two girls into something they were not prepared to handle. I do not question the sentences of the judge, which were entirely fair, in my opinion.

"However, it did occur to me that if we were to agree to Stark's deal, our children might then not have to serve their sentences, or would be subject to sharply reduced sentences. As much as I would wish this from a father's point of view, it behooves me to say at this point that I would not go along with this deal, even if it did result in much lighter or non-existent sentences for our children.

"FatLand is a young country. We are soon to celebrate our 25th year of Territorial Sovereignty. One hundred years from now, FatLanders—perhaps some of us here, even, considering our wonderfully low mortality rate—" Alvin smiled and the rest of the Board members smiled, "will remember what we decided here tonight. They will remember whether we decided to make a deal with a completely unscrupulous person who tried to do away with his honorable competition by crass manipulation and tried to wangle and wiggle his way out of a heinous crime thereby, or whether we stood proud and firm and did not compromise with him, even though such a compromise might have resulted in less difficulty and anxiety and yes, suffering, for at least some of us.

"As Ed said, the people in the Safe House did not act as they did only for us to give in to what this person desires, which is no less than the eventual destruction of FatLand. They are counting on us not only to provide for their personal safety, which of course we would do in any case, but to stand true to the principles for which they risked their lives.

"Even though it might benefit me and my children and my wife and the dear people in the Safe House in the short run, compromise with Winston Stark is out of the question. This is a test of what Fat-Land and of what we, the Board of FatLand, are made of. Such tests come along perhaps once in a generation, and they shape the destinies and lives of succeeding generations. This is the test of our time, of our generation.

"Let us stand up and hold true to what we believe at our core and what we know to be right. Let the moral compass guide us so that Fat-Landers of the future can say, 'They stood up for what they created.'"

After the applause ceased, Margaret said, "Before the next Board member speaks, Detective Sergeant Leffler would like to address us. He was supposed to be here earlier, but he got a little held up. Are you ready now to talk to us, Sergeant?"

"I'm ready," Detective Leffler said, taking a few breaths. "Traffic along Gleason Avenue was rough."

"Have a sip of iced tea," Margaret said, pushing the pitcher and a blue glass cup over to Leffler.

"Later," he said. He looked down at the well-made but unadorned pine table. "The first thing I want and need to say is that Winston Stark has, in effect, a private army at his disposal, and weapons and air vehicles to match. The second thing is that he is beginning to be unpopular in Colorado because GymNotTrim serves rich, satisfying snacks and hors d'oeuvres, and Complete Fitness does not.

"The third thing is that there is a deep swell of discontent building on the Other Side, and that as heroic as you all are, it may not be the best time to send your kids there to learn a salutary lesson."

"What do you think will happen?" Margaret asked.

"Can't say for sure. But you can feel it in the air. People were going crazy quietly for a while. Now some strange things are happening. People are seizing the houses of rich people who were away and having parties and eating their food. The rich people were always the ones who could get away with having good things on the table for parties because they could pay the Non-Approved Food fines and taxes."

"That's why the guy at the Colorado checkpoint was so happy to get that Dutch apple pie," Ava said. "He would never have been able to afford the tax."

"And you're going to be seeing more of that," Vance said.

"If Stark's getting so unpopular, which doesn't surprise me," Sandor said, "and this is also part of a more general discontent, maybe with the proper stimulation people will rebel against the Pro-Health Laws and they'll be history."

"It's possible," Leffler conceded. "The problem is that before that happens, Stark can be nasty in a major way, and especially to FatLand."

"I think," Margaret said, "that it is time for me to stop hiding and become courageous and see Stark."

Chapter 9

Margaret

STRANGELY ENOUGH, Margaret felt quite calm as the car driven by a subordinate of Stark's sped up the freeway leading to a mountain road. She was calm because she doubted Stark could think of anything new or interesting to say to her. *He likes manipulating people and watching them fall into his little trips and hooks,* she thought, then dismissed him from her mind and let herself melt into the scenery.

The car turned onto the mountain road.

Snow clung to the mountains at this altitude, although spring was starting in FatLand and at lower altitudes in Colorado. The trip had lasted about five hours. She had not been hungry at all, but now she was starting to feel a bit peckish.

The car turned onto a narrow and winding road. Not a fan of heights—which was why she had let Ava do the skiing for their "Skiing in FatLand" feature—Margaret noted that the car was still traveling almost as fast as it had on the highway. *Is he planning to kill me by having someone push me out or having the car fall over the mountain?* she started to wonder.

The car finally stopped in front of what resembled less a house than a fortress, complete with castle and moat. *Didn't think Stark was that fanciful,* she thought, amused for the first time during the trip.

"Please follow me," the driver said. He took her overnight bag and walked through a gate into the central entrance of the castle. She followed a few steps behind him, looking around her as a good reporter should. *This is starting to be interesting,* she thought.

After "checking in" with a concierge-like woman who was attired in the kind of navy suit Ava had described in her series on Sandor's trial, the driver opened a door to reveal a dizzyingly beautiful room done in white and light blue, with windows open to the snowy mountains.

"Please be seated," the driver said. "Mr. Stark will be with you short-ly." He pointed at a tray. "Cocoa, coffee, fruit, cheese, flatbreads and pastries. You will dine later, but Mr. Stark felt you might be a bit hun-gry after the trip."

"How thoughtful of him," Margaret said, trying to keep the sarcasm out of her voice.

"He can be quite thoughtful," the driver said, and left.

Although still somewhat hungry, Margaret stood and paced. The long narrow room made her feel as if she were in a fairy-tale tower, bordered by mountains and perhaps, she added to herself, some snow monsters, abominable and otherwise. She hated to grant Stark the power to make her enjoy anything, but the lofty, dreamy appeal of the room overwhelmed her senses.

She reached for the pot of cocoa and poured some into a gently fluted white china cup. She sat down in the chair nearest the room-length window and sipped. When she had had her fill of the nearest mountain, she stood up and helped herself to one of the flatbreads with a square of baby Gouda.

Then she remembered that most people in Colorado would not be able to afford one fifth of the food that had been assembled on the tray in front of her, and she felt better, more back to her fighting self. She would keep this in mind, she thought, when Stark made his entrance.

Night entered the room as the mountains grew darker. *Wish he'd get here already,* she thought as she sampled a piece of apple strudel. Then she fell asleep.

MARGARET AWOKE to find herself in a sumptuous bedroom, morn-ing sun pouring through the windows. She pushed aside the thick gold velvet quilt coverlet and looked around, trying to figure out how she had ended up in this room, and when, and why.

At least her overnight bag was there. She checked to see if her Pod was still in it. It was.

She also checked the other side of the huge circular bed. (Hadn't circular beds been fashionable about sixty years ago?) No wrinkling or ruffling there. So she had been the only inhabitant.

Obvious question, she thought as her gaze alighted on the tea and bagels with cream cheese, lox, tomatoes, capers, and lemons perched charmingly on a bed tray. Where was Stark? Had he been delayed? And if so, why?

Time for thought after breakfast, she decided. Then she remembered that she had fallen asleep after eating a piece of strudel.

Taking her mind back to last night, she granted that she had been rather tired after waiting and could easily have fallen asleep on her own without any additional assistance. She also admitted that she was making excuses to eat this most tempting breakfast, which was accompanied, she now saw, by miniature almond and chocolate croissants and little chocolate and raspberry donuts. Homemade, too—she could tell.

Should she podmail someone in case she fell asleep in the middle of a bagel, she wondered? But something told her that would not be the case. *Oh well, here goes,* she thought, and crafted a half-bagel sandwich.

She bit into it. *Delicious,* she thought, and felt no falling or sleepy sensations.

She continued to eat while her mind searched for a solution to her removal from the other room and to Stark's absence.

Chapter 10

Ava

FROM CRISIS TO CRISIS, Ava thought as she podmailed the Board about the latest turn of events. The first one to podmail back was Sandor from the Safe House.

"I suggest that we try to contact Vance," Sandor said.

"I'd like to run it by Leffler first," Ava said.

"All right."

Reevie, whom she called instead of podmailing, said, "Oh God, poor Marge. How did she sound?"

"In the podmail, she sounded more amused than anything else."

"Thank goodness. You going to call Leffler?"

"Yes, but mostly so he knows we're contacting Vance."

"Vance?" Reevie sounded dubious. "You sure?"

"He'll at least know where Stark is. From then we can figure out what to do next."

Joann said, "Slimy, but he'd know, all right."

"Yeah, that's what I figure."

"Ed wants to storm the mountain."

"Charming," Ava said, "but that place is a fortress, according to Marge."

AVA WAS ABOUT TO CONTACT Leffler when a new podmail came in.

"Margaret is in no danger," it read. "As long as you don't try to be foolish and rescue her. In any case we could take out FatLand's entire airpower with one device, so don't even think of it."

158

The podmail was unsigned. Ava traced its path to Alaska.

Good lord, she thought, and podmailed Leffler. His response was almost immediate. "Don't do anything until I've had a chance to trace the mail."

Five minutes later he podmailed her back. "That podmail is from Alaska," he said. "But Margaret's is from Colorado."

"Hmm," Ava typed. "So at least she hasn't been moved in her sleep or anything like that."

"I'm going to get hold of Vance," Leffler responded. "I know you don't like him, but he'll be very useful."

"I trust your professional judgment," Ava said.

Chapter 11

Dara

DARA BLINKED AT THE PODMAIL in front of her. Then she read it. She poured more vanilla and spice tea into her cup, sipped it, and read the podmail again.

Hey, Dara—
Yeah, it's Drew. Long time no see. Miss you, sweetie.

Neat trick, getting your flame out of here. I'm sure you were the brains behind it. No one else would have been able to pull it off.

So, hon, this is what I wanted to say to you.

I know you're hot for Sandor. I am sure he's hot for you, too. But see, I wouldn't trust him too far. He always has several schemes going on in that two-timing head of his. I know because I've worked with him in the past.

Remember the time when they wanted to shore up the fronts of the buildings on Winters Street, and then they found a few cost overruns? That was your honey. He pushed to give the contract to a buddy of his who decided to be generous with his workers. Too generous.

But, you say, that's just work. Men act that way in professional and occupational dealings.

Let me give you a different example.

Why do you think Sandor never used to stay in Board meetings too long when Margaret was there? No, it wasn't because she has body odor. It's because he's been hot for her for a while. Don't you remember the way he used to look when he would mention her name? Sorry to have to tell you this, and I know those Fat-Land hypocrites would never mention such a thing. They like happy endings, even if the endings have to be twisted around to appear happy.

I know it was damned brave of you to arrange for Sandor to be kidnapped and put in one of the Safe Houses. But we can get him at any time. We know by now exactly where he is.

If I were you, I would take the rest of that cruise he so conveniently created an excuse to put off. Yeah, I know that hot dancer died, but it wasn't necessary for you guys to run home that quickly. Nothing would have happened if you'd stayed longer and taken in more sights and sun.

What's more, if you take the cruise, I will gladly pay for it and accompany you. We had a few dates and laughs once upon a time—do you remember? I'd like to get to know the real Dara, the one who lurks so mysteriously and coolly and interestingly behind those glasses. The one who seems reserved and removed, but who glides like white fire up the bed.

I miss you, babe. We never should have let the acquaintance slip. And believe me, you deserve someone better than Two-Timing Forman.

So let me know what you think. I'll be waiting to hear from you.

Yours remembering the good times,
Drew

DARA GLANCED once more at the podmail. Then she forwarded it to every member of the Board, except for Sandor.

AT THE END OF THE DAY, after finishing her shift in the hospital, Dara walked over to the Safe House and let herself in with the card.

Sandor was sitting at the kitchen table, as were Crystal and Shermaine. They were talking with Louann, who was in the middle of fixing dinner. It seemed a happy, peaceful scene, the kind could almost serve as an advertisement for FatLand living.

"Would you mind if I had a word with you?" she said to Sandor after smiling hello to Crystal and Shermaine.

"Of course, babe," he said, and rose from the table.

"I received this early today," she said.

He read the podmail and started to laugh. "That's rich," he said. "Guess old Stark simply can't take no or goodbye for an answer. It humiliates him. So Drew does his bidding. Did you ever like him?"

"I didn't really think a lot about him," Dara said. "He asked me out a couple of times, so I went. Then he found other fish to fry." She looked at him. "Did you ever like Margaret?"

Sandor began to laugh again. "If one likes people one is afraid of and doesn't want to bump into a lot. I mean, I feel a lot differently about her now, but she wouldn't have been on my dance card formerly, if you know what I mean."

"So he's trying to sow dissension in the ranks, and to have us desert you?"

"In the worst way."

"But somehow it also tells me that Margaret is all right. I don't think he would write about her that way if she weren't."

"Agreed," Sandor said. "Did you forward this to the Board members?"

"I sure did."

"I guess they'll call another meeting. Let's see what we all come up with."

Chapter 12

Margaret

MY DEAR FRIENDS,

First of all, please be assured that I am quite well. The essentials—food, shelter, clothing—have been provided abundantly and even luxuriously, especially when one considers what the average citizen in Colorado ingests, possesses and wears. My surroundings are incredibly lovely, with rooms that seems to melt into the mountains nearby.

However, an interesting aspect of my time here thus far is that Stark and his assistants and co-conspirators are not here. Since they have communicated with me by screen but not by podmail, I have no way of knowing where they actually are. Something says "Europe" to me, but that may be way off.

I myself have not seen any weapons—at least not yet—but the shape and appearance of this place seem tailor-made for producing great quantities of them. The place resembles a fortress—in some aspects, medieval, in others, quite contemporary.

Two days after I arrived here I was greeted, after lunch, by the appearance of Stark and Harris on the screen. Winston looks surprisingly well for his years and lack of scruples. Harris, however, looks as if the subordinate role does not really suit him. He seemed ill-at-ease and sulky in some kind of grey muddy tweed.

"Hello, Margaret," Winston said.

I nodded and said hello back. No reason to lose decorum here, I thought.

"So how do you like my little mountain home?"

I said that I thought it was quite lovely.

"Good," he said. "Because you're going to be there for a while. A long while. Maybe forever."

I asked how he had arrived at that conclusion.

"Simple," he said. "I want you to be there. I don't want to let you out. Thus you will be there as long as I wish you to be there."

"But what," I asked, "if I happen to have other preferences?"

"Then I would suggest that you amend them," he said.

"Why do you wish me to be here?" I asked.

"Simple," he said. "You are necessary to me. You are not necessary to anyone else."

"I beg to differ," I said. "I do have certain professional obligations to fulfill."

"If you mean that paper of yours," he said, "Ava and the others can run it. I've been following it continuously, as you know. It's a pretty smooth-running machine by now."

"It sounds as if you wish to repossess it."

"Not at all. I want to possess only one thing in FatLand, and it is now in front of me on the screen."

"Very flattering," I said. "As usual, you seek to hide me away somewhere. Still ashamed of your desire? And why did you send a helicopter to harass the people in the Safe House?"

"That was fun," Winston said. "Pure fun, nothing else. I thought they might miss being chased."

"You have a strange sense of fun, Winston," I said.

"Sometimes," he said. Then he looked almost contrite, if you can imagine Winston looking contrite. "Listen, Margaret," he said, "I know I've been a heel. But I still care for you deeply. I really think about nothing else. If you tell me you'll be my mistress forever, I will drop charges against Sandor and that ridiculous imitation of a corporation he has."

"Your wife," I said. "Assuming that you still have a wife. What about her?"

"What about her?" Winston asked. "She has her uses."

"And I have mine."

"You are indeed useful," he said. "In many ways."

"Tell you what, Winston," I said. "If you consent to drop any charges against Sandor and to stop harassing the inhabitants of the Safe House permanently, I will become your mistress. But you know, FatLanders—myself included—are still very angry at you over Amiyah."

"Oh, yes," he said. "The Egyptian dancer. Shame about that."

"It is a shame," I said. "You are the one who called for her removal. And we know that."

"She was a two-timing bitch anyway," he said. "She would never have been faithful to Ava. I saved Ava a lot of heartache."

"You used to be more suave and charming," I said.

"I can become so again," he said. "If you give me some incentive."

"I don't know if I wish to give you anything."

"Give me a chance to prove to you what kind of lover I can be," he said. "Before you reject me outright."

"You wouldn't have the vaguest notion of what kind of lover I would want," I said. Nights spent with my FatLand friends discussing exactly this subject sent their breezes through my brain again. "I want a lover who would kiss and caress very slowly every part of my long, thick body. And some nights, that is all he would do. I would want him to worship every part of me with his hands and tongue."

"Oh God," he said. "You're already starting to get me hot. I was imagining you spread out on the sheets without any clothes on."

"Before we start having pod sex," I said, "I suggest that we meet in person."

"Don't you see," he said in a lower tone of voice. "I can't come back there. Not now. Not ever. The State of Colorado has indicted me."

"For something done in FatLand?"

"No. They can't rule on that. But they said I misrepresented the facts when I accused Sandor of reneging. So the case against Sandor is on appeal."

"Very interesting," I said. "In that case, how would we be lovers?"

"On the screen," he said.

I tried not to laugh. "Winston," I said, "we are both in our forties. Screen sex is for younger people."

"Usually it is," he said. "But I can't come back there."

"And I notice," I said, "that you are not exactly begging me to join you. Thus I must conclude that your wife is with you there, wherever you are. And thus I am to be your secret mistress?"

"You don't have a choice," Winston said.

"Is that so?" I said.

"Even if they sent a helicopter for you, we could blot out any seeable image of this place. Do you know how?"

"How?"

"We make our own clouds."

This did impress me, in spite of everything. "Neat," I said.

"Go down to the Action Room sometime and have Dave show you."

"Who's Dave?"

"Your driver. But actually he's my right hand man there."

"I will," I said.

"And Margaret?"

"Yes?"

"From now on, you check in on the screen every three hours during the day. Is that clear?"

"Oh, quite clear," I said.

He seemed disappointed that I was not screaming or outwardly resisting, or both. Winston likes his victims to do both, I think. Gives the control games added spice. You could tell from what he said next. "So you're okay with being here for a while?"

"As you said," I pointed out, "I don't really have a choice."

But within these parameters, I can do a lot of exploring. Since he's willing to have Dave show me the Action Room, Winston is obviously not loathe to my learning more about the place. As for the screen sex—well, let's see. He's more into the idea of my being helpless right now than our having screen sex, from what I can sense.

So the upshot and downshot of this mail is, especially if you are having a Board meeting: Don't do anything quite yet. I am not in any danger. I am thoroughly amused. And I think we might learn some interesting things.

"SHE SEEMS PRETTY DEFINITE," Joann said at the Board meeting the next day.

"Quite," Ava agreed.

They were meeting in the Safe House so Sandor could participate without anyone having to worry about his safety or whereabouts. "I think we should still think about a possible rescue," Sandor said.

"Agreed," Dara said.

"But not one that would put her at risk," Reevie said. "And if they can make clouds there to shield themselves, it might be a while before we could figure out where she was anyway."

"She seems pretty safe," Alvin said.

"For now," Dara said. "Let's keep monitoring her podmails."

"Let's vote on that," Reevie said. She was Chair that night.

The vote was unanimous to keep a close watch on Margaret's podmails and to come up with a plan to intervene if necessary.

Chapter 13

Jesse

DEAR MOM AND DAD,

I've been doing a lot of thinking lately. I know that Winston Stark's disappearance might have let me off the hook in terms of my sentence as an accomplice. But I feel as if my life has little or no meaning here now. Maybe that's one of the reasons I agreed to help with what I thought was scaring someone who was completely innocent.

I have decided to go to Colorado, as my sentence dictated. The only difference is that I will definitely see you at least every few months. And I'll be with Mira and I'll help her in whatever way I can.

I didn't really see what there was for me to do in FatLand, somehow. Everything seems so final, kind of dead end here. Everyone is defined by the time they're 25. But I feel as if I'm still waiting to grow up, to define what I am and am not.

And don't worry about my losing weight. I'll just keep going to GymNotTrim, ha ha. That way I can exercise but keep fed quite well.

I'm glad you guys launched the exchange program with Colorado. I think it was long overdue. Who knows? Maybe if they'd had that program when I and Aimee and Jenna were growing up, we wouldn't have felt so restless and trapped.

Another good thing about my going to Colorado is that I'll probably find out how advanced and free and tolerant living in FatLand is in comparison. Mira was mentioning this in her podmails, you know. But I will see for myself, which is what I've wanted for a long time.

I think this experience will make me grow as a human being. I will be able to find out who I am and what I am, and what I am not. The next time you see me, which I hope will be in not too long—at least for my birthday—I will have learned a lot about many things. And hopefully I will be a better, more complete person because of it.

I will miss you terribly, but I will be with Mira, so that will help a little. Don't worry about me.

Keep on doing exactly what you do and going to Board meetings and holding FatLand together. It will be good to know that some things stay the same, no matter where I go or how long I'm away.

Love,
Your Son Jesse

Chapter 14

Sandor

STARK DISAPPEARS; CLANCY FOUND
TORELLI DECIDES TO EXILE HIMSELF VOLUNTARILY
BY AVA BRYER

ONE OF MARGARET CLANCY'S favorite Irish folk tunes floats over the soundwaves as she smiles into the screen. But the editor of *The FatLand Free News* is not in FatLand; she's in Colorado.

We are not at liberty to reveal her location, but she tells us that she is somewhere in the mountains in a beautiful, luxurious house. She also informs us that she is healthy and maintaining a keen interest in what takes place in her new surroundings.

She will tell us more as she explores her new environment. We will keep you posted.

IN ANOTHER DEVELOPMENT, what might have been a grave situation was alleviated by the disappearance of Winston Stark, who had accused Sandor Forman of FatLand of reneging on a contract to merge his physical wellness firm GymNotTrim with Stark's Complete Fitness group.

Stark had been accused of requesting the death of the Egyptian dancer Amiyah and would have been tried in absentia in FatLand.

"DOES THAT MEAN WE'RE FREE?" Shermaine asked Sandor over breakfast that morning as they looked at the headlines on the kitchen screen.

"Seems that way to me," Sandor said. "But I wouldn't ever trust Stark completely not to pull something."

"What could he do now?" Crystal asked. "You told us that Margaret said he was out of the country."

"He may be out of the country," Sandor said, passing Patty a bagel."But he still has people here. He could ask them to do anything. That's how the whole thing started."

"Are they just going to leave Margaret there?" Crystal asked as she buttered a slice of rye toast.

"That's what she requested."

"You think she'll be safe?"

"As long as Stark thinks he can have fun and games with her."

"So FatLand doesn't have to go to war?" Louann commented from where she was heating up more coffee.

"Not yet. Hopefully not ever," Sandor said. He beamed as Dara came into the kitchen. "Hello, babe. Have some challah french toast."

"Maybe a slice," Dara agreed. She handed something to Sandor.

"A love note," Crystal said.

"Of course," Dara said, and poured maple syrup on the slice of challah french toast.

Sandor put the note in his pocket and continued to eat and talk. A few minutes later he and Dara excused themselves from the table to the winks and grins of the rest.

"We'll have to tell them about this," Dara said. "But as a member of the Board, you're supposed to see it first."

Sandor read:

Communication from Margaret over podmail. Two prisons in the United States of America started to riot this morning over the Pro-Health Laws. The inmates arrested because of their non-compliance with the Laws started to demand more and better food. The other inmates joined in. Margaret thinks it's going to spread. Will keep you posted. Meeting tonight at the Torellis'.

"Wow," he said.

"Yeah."

They both looked at the note. "I don't want you to go back there," she said. "Ever."

"I will go only if you can come with me," Sandor said.

"Is that a promise?"

"Yes."

Chapter 15

The FatLand Board

"EXTRAORDINARY TIMES ARE UPON US," Joann said at the beginning of the next Board meeting. "Extraordinary times call for extraordinary measures.

"The riots that started in two prisons on the Other Side have spread all over the country. We now have word that there are demonstrations in support of the prisoners and against the Pro-Health Laws in every major city, and many minor ones.

"The question here, of course, is what we can do to assist our sisters and brothers on the Other Side. Do we send letters? Do we demonstrate in support? Do we sing? We have already started to print articles in support of the prisoners and the demonstrators. What else is to be done?

"I am going to go around the room. Sandor, you wish to start first?"

Sandor stood. "Judging by what I saw when I was on the Other Side recently,"he said, "I think that the people who are challenging the Pro-Health Laws—whether in prisons or by demonstrating or by refusing to abide by the statutes and stipulations—are going to need a lot more from us than articles and letters. That's why I wanted Shermaine, Crystal, and Patty to attend this meeting." He indicated the presence of the three women by inclining his head in their direction.

"Your point is well-taken," Joann agreed. "Shermaine, Crystal, Patty— we are looking to you for input of any kind. We would also like to have your take on what's going on."

"These are exciting times," Crystal said. "But people get killed in exciting times.

"I am seriously afraid that the police in the USA are not going to be easy on the prisoners or the demonstrators. Courtesy of Mega Pharmacies and Mega Lifestyle Agencies who want those Pro-Health Laws to stay right in place so they can keep selling their meds to captive consumers who are forced to be on them.

"Patty and I were forced to take what are in effect megastimulants for three years. I did not get a good night's sleep until I came here with Sandor and was able to go off the megastimulants. And for the record, the megastimulants did not even make me lose weight and they increased my blood pressure.

"But worse, I am even more worried about the sentences judges will impose. They are going to stretch every one, as they did with Sandor, who is not even a citizen of the USA. The prisons will be ten times as crowded—and they are crowded already—with people whose only crimes were to defy the Pro-Health Laws. That will be ten times more people starved or force-medicated.

"You keep thinking that things can't get any worse, that people will rebel, that some high-minded senators will decide that it is time to void the Pro-Health Laws. But the Senate voted overwhelmingly in this present session to extend the Pro-Health Laws for five years more. You can just imagine who is paying them or giving them contributions."

"Sounds like we'll have to do for a lot of them what we did for Sandor," Shermaine said. "I don't know how many FatLand can take in, but if you can sponsor U.S. emigrants and send them to countries where they can live without being starved and force-medicated—"

"How to send them, though? " Reevie said. "They'd be watching all the borders." She looked over to Alvin.

"Sounds like we need an Underground Railroad," he said. "People could drive them from one Safe House to another across the continental U.S. And then get them out of the country, if necessary."

"In case some of you were not aware of the fact," Sandor said, "GymNotTrim buildings across the USA are now serving as Safe Houses."

Everyone looked at Sandor. Dara looked down. "It was her idea," he said, pointing to Dara. "But FatAndProud helped, as they did before." He glanced at Crystal, Shermaine, and Patty.

"Do people live in them?" Ed asked.

"If they have to," Sandor said. "Many people stay as long as they can or need to, depending on their circumstances. We are prepared to tell any police personnel that these people are exercising. Since exercising is looked on as an obligation on the Other Side these days, anyone who asked would approve, no doubt.

"But we have not had even one inquiry. That in itself helps. But of course even all the GymNotTrims can only hold and support so many people at a given time. Listening to what you've all been saying, though, gives me an idea. If we can keep using the GymNotTrims as Safe Houses, and moving people from one to the other, we can in effect have that Underground Railroad of which Alvin spoke. We could drive some into FatLand and send the rest to different countries."

"I had another podmail from Margaret this morning," Ava said. She read: "'What I suggest is that this house serve as a Safe House.' So she was already thinking along those lines."

"How about this?" Reevie said. "We drive people from the nearest GymNotTrims to wherever Margaret is. We then get people to drive them over the border from Colorado or to the airport nearest to that house." She looked around to Shermaine and the other two FatAnd-Proud members. "Is that doable?"

"Sure," Crystal said.

"When you're on those so-called weight-loss drugs constantly," Patty said, "you have lots of nervous energy. Of course, it's that or surgery, so many people choose the pills instead. We have loads of energy among our friends." She laughed. "Of course there are a few ways to fool the drug enforcers, but they're risky. You eat garlic, I think. It makes the test results positive. Yecchh.

"Anyway, lots of FatAndProud people would drive them. No problem."

Chapter 16

The Johnsons

"JENNA WANTS TO DO SOMETHING CRAZY, Mom," Aimee said.

"What now?" Reevie asked. She was typing and looking at the clock. There would be another Board meeting at 8, and she was presiding.

"She wants to be a driver from Margaret's Safe House to FatLand for the people who are escaping."

"Did she tell you this?"

"She emailed a friend about it."

"So how did you find out?"

"She's my friend, too. Sherla."

"Sherla told you?"

"Yes."

"Was Jenna planning to tell us?"

"Yes, but I wanted you to know. I think it's really dangerous."

"It *is* dangerous," Reevie agreed. She stopped typing. "Do you think we should stop her?"

"I don't know."

"Did you want to go with her?"

"I didn't want to go there to drive people," Aimee said. "I just wanted to see what the Other Side was like. That's why we used to go to The Laurels."

"Why do you think Jenna wants to drive people?"

"I think she feels guilty for what happened to Amiyah."

"You don't think she cares about the people who are in danger now and who need help?"

"I think she wants to atone."

"If she were presented with other ways to atone, do you think she would change her mind?"

"I don't know. Jenna always wanted to be a hero, like the people in the Safe House."

"Would that be so terrible?"

"Yes, if she dies or goes to jail there."

Reevie said, "Does she want to speak tonight?"

"Yes."

AIMEE KNOCKED on the bedroom door. Jenna answered. "I wanted to talk," Aimee said.

"Go ahead."

Jenna didn't invite Aimee to sit down, so she stood. "Do you know what happens to you if you end up in a prison on the other side?"

"I am completely aware of that," Jenna answered.

"You always wanted to sacrifice your life for something," Aimee said. "Guess you have the chance now."

"That's my business," Jenna said. "You just can't stand the fact that you look like a coward now."

"I look like a sane person," Aimee said. She rushed out of the room and ran down the stairs. She went out the front door, slammed it shut, and started off very fast, not caring where she walked.

"I'VE CALLED THE POLICE," Reevie said quietly. "They didn't have any clues."

"It's almost eight now," Alvin said. "The members are due any second."

"I know."

Reevie was on the first step of the stairs when the phone rang. It was Ava. Reevie began "Do you— "

"You can relax, Reeves," Ava said. "She's here with me."

"Thank God," Reevie said, swallowing. "Is she—?"

"She's fine. I think we'll skip the Board meeting tonight and I'll let her talk herself out."

"Thank you for saving her," Reevie said, a tear hanging on her long lashes.

"She saved herself," Ava said. "I'll call you tomorrow."

Chapter 17

Margaret

"DAVE," MARGARET SAID as she ensconced herself in the Sky Room with some Mallomars and very hot tea with cream, no sugar, "can Winston ever come back?"

Dave laughed. He reached for a Mallomar and sat down next to Margaret. "Not unless he wants to be hounded by police from several states and your territory."

Margaret said, "My territory? We wouldn't hurt a fly."

Dave laughed more.

"Dave," Margaret said again, "Have another Mallomar. I am thinking seriously of putting this house under cover. People would land here by navigation only. Then we would fly them or drive them to FatLand. What do you say to that?"

"I say," Dave said, leaning down and putting his arm around Margaret, "that Winston is not here. You are here. I want you desperately. Should we make sure all the screens are off or would it turn you on to have him watch?"

"Maybe later," Margaret said, reaching for Dave's lips with her own.

IT HAD BEEN SO LONG, Margaret thought a couple of hours later. She watched Dave as he slept. She had debated whether to put something in his tea, but was glad it hadn't been necessary after all. She had almost but not quite forgotten how quickly many men fell asleep after.

The very convenient thing, she decided as she went down to the

Networking Room, as Dave called it, was that most women did not fall asleep after.

Chapter 18

Jesse

JESSE DROVE AS SLOWLY AND CAREFULLY as he could over the leg of the Underground Anti-Dieting Railroad, or UADR, that he had been assigned.

It was the most difficult leg—from the eastern border of Colorado to what was now Margaret's Safe House. But a spring snowstorm had lessened visibility to such an extent that he could not even see the road in front of him. He figured that the only thing to do under such circumstances was to stop and buzz Margaret to warn her that he was delayed.

As he got out the podphone and one-clicked her number, a speeding truck crashed into the van and knocked it down the pass. It landed so hard that the entire top of the van crumbled against the lowest slope like so much tin.

Jesse's podphone emitted a faint signal, then went dead.

The snow whirled in eddies as the wind whistled and moaned through the twists of the mountain pass and the crumpled van. Then silence reigned.

THEY HAD COME from all corners of FatLand. Hushed, saddened, reverent, they watched as the black car draped in green, yellow, and purple—FatLand's colors—wound its way slowly, majestically to the gravesite. When it stopped, four FatLanders, two women, two men—members of the Honor Guard—stooped and bore the coffin aloft. They hoisted it, then deposited it slowly into the space reserved for it.

A strong April breeze lifted the scents and particles of columbines and aspens into the crowd. Ed Torelli took the microphone.

"Thank you for coming to my son's funeral," he said, his voice rough but not breaking. "Jesse always loved this time of year. He used to run several miles at a time with his friends.

"My son died in the service of the noblest cause imaginable, the drive to liberate those under the yoke of the Pro-Health Laws, those who had gone to prison because of those unjust rules. I am very proud of him. His soul is free now of the desperation and wish to atone that marked it recently. Jesse, if your soul can hear me, you have atoned in the proudest and best way possible, in trying to save others. But we will leave that to God to work out.

"Jesse always wanted to be a hero, but felt there was no place for heroes in FatLand. He was wrong; He is our hero. But in a way he was right, too. For so many years we painted ourselves as refugees from injustice, which we were, as are the people Jesse was trying so hard to save. But we have become more than refugees. We have become trailblazers and pioneers, people determined to live their own way in the face of unending pressure and difficulties.

"We did carve out a haven here for people who were persecuted because of their body shapes and those who wanted to stop such persecution. But we must now accept and emphasize our own heroism in fighting this persecution. That is what my son's soul wanted and was crying out for. But we did not offer it because we did not understand.

"Jesse, besides dying in a heroic cause, you pointed the way for us to see and believe ourselves heroes. We ourselves may once have internalized the belief that fat people can be happy, but not heroes. We were wrong. We are all heroes, but more so because Jesse showed us the way to be heroes.

"However, besides leaving a legacy of fighting to give others their freedom, Jesse left another legacy that may prove just as or even more important. Before he left on his last mission, he created a web page that talks about FatLand and invites communities on the Other Side to form Diet-Free Zones with our help.

"If enough communities on the Other Side form Diet-Free Zones, untouchable by the Pro-Health Laws, the Fat Acceptance Revolution will be won in many places, maybe even the majority of areas on the Other Side. This is our next task—to help people on the Other Side say a polite—if they wish—but firm 'No, thank you!' to people who would tell them how to eat and think and live their lives.

"Freedom will reign once again in what should have been the Land of the Free, but was coopted and stolen away by large conglomerates and government complicity.

"Jesse, we miss you terribly. We failed you, but you did not fail us. Be assured that your debt has not only been paid with interest, but has been erased, so that many citizens we help today and in the future will be in your debt. You are a hero to us, to all FatLanders and to all those in future generations who will reap your gift of free living and thinking."

Ed picked up the spade, dug and tossed the first shower of earth into the grave. Joann, Alvin and Reevie followed.

Sandor picked up the mic. "In the memory of Jesse, and in dedication to a brave woman who is very much with us in spirit but cannot be here with us today, I would like to announce that Dara and I have decided to take over Jesse's route on the Anti-Dieting Underground Railroad."

There were a few gasps, but most of the crowd remained quiet.

"Jesse, you will not have died in vain. We miss you and honor you. Rest safe and proud."

Chapter 19

Sandor & Dara

"I'D LIKE TO WELCOME YOU ALL to the Anti-Dieting Underground Railroad." The woman stayed in shadow, but her voice was powerful and confident. "Today I will acquaint you with the procedures you will use to drive or fly your escapees to the next safe point."

Sandor noted that she was dressed in something resembling a space suit. Then he realized it was a kind of ski outfit.

"Please watch." The smartpoint presentation showed maps and driving techniques in fog, snow, slush and freezing rain. It also provided methods of camouflage, avoiding contact with Pro-Health Officers, and ways to bribe them. "Now," the woman announced, "we will role play. Please select partners. There are an even number of people in the room, so there shouldn't be any problem. Remember, you are to use at least one of the techniques shown in the film. As a reward—" Dara felt the wink even if she couldn't see it—"we will go to GymNotTrim after this session."

"Did you authorize that?" Dara whispered.

"Yep," Sandor whispered back.

As the woman wenr around the room listening to the role-playing exercise, Dara and Sandor pretended that she was trying to bribe him.

"Very good," the woman said. "Dara, you played the 'wounded waif' extremely effectively."

"Do we know you?" Dara asked.

"Yes," the woman said. "Think of this training exercise as my tribute to my brother."

"Mira," Sandor said softly.

"I couldn't get back for the funeral, although I very much wanted to," Mira said. "Every day I think of him."

"He was a hero," Sandor said.

"In a way I'm glad he died as he did," Mira said. "Jesse always wanted to be a hero. He finally had the chance."

"We're doing more about honoring fat heroes now," Sandor said.

"And heroines," Dara added. "We should have done it before. We didn't realize—" She stopped. "You're a hero, too. Your parents are so proud."

"Thanks," Mira said. As she walked away, Dara noticed that a tear had found its way down Mira's cheek. But no more followed.

"Do you feel ready?" Dara asked Sandor.

"Not quite yet," he admitted.

"You will have several short practice simulations," Mira announced, as if she had anticipated their diffidence. "Only when we judge that you are ready will we send you out."

"Will we have podtalkers?" a woman from Vale asked.

"The way we do it," Mira said, "is if you wish to have podtalkers, we will give them to you. They do heighten your risk of being found out and arrested. But we realize they can be quite useful. So we give you that option.

"And now," she announced, "a word from one of our leaders."

"I would like to greet everyone assembled here tonight." The voice came sweet, strong and clear over the speakers. "I'm so glad you all have volunteered to drive these runs—"

"Margaret!" Dara whispered to Sandor.

"Yeah," he said, taking her hand. "She sounds great." He squeezed it. "That bastard Harris," he said with barely concealed anger.

"You knew?"

"She told me." Sandor swung her hand back and forth. "Don't give him another thought," he said almost hoarsely. "Don't waste your energy on him. Don't even waste mind cells on him."

"I won't," Dara said, feeling as if a great burden had been lifted from her heart. She continued to listen to Margaret describe the last run of the route, the one for which she and Sandor would be responsible.

A late spring snow started to fall.

Chapter 20

The Johnsons

"I MISS THEM SO MUCH," Reevie said, a few tears falling.

It was evening in FatLand. "I would say go over to the Safe House, but they've all left to volunteer for the Anti-Diet Underground Railroad," Alvin said, putting an arm around Reevie.

"Should we volunteer?"

"Some of us have to stay here and help the folks who come here," Alvin said. "Can't all go running to the Other Side. Or there won't be a refuge."

"I hope Jenna will podmail tomorrow."

"I'm sure she will if she can."

"I hope someone doesn't hijack Aimee's plane."

"Reevie, prayer helps more than worry."

"You are so right," Reevie agreed. They both got on their knees on the deep blue swirls of the art rug warming the study. They clasped their hands and vented their hopes and worries.

"Now," Alvin said, "doesn't that feel better?"

"Yep. I wonder where Aimee is now."

Alvin looked at his watch. "Judging by the time and the time difference, probably somewhere over Europe. They're supposed to arrive 10 AM our time."

"She'll be tired," Reevie said.

"Don't worry," Alvin said. "Ava will get them both into a cab and straight to the hotel. She's so good at that."

"She is," Reevie agreed. They both looked up at the cloudy night sky as if they could see beyond the clouds to where Aimee and Jenna continued on their respective journeys.

Jenna

FINALLY.

Sometimes it takes an upheaval for people to discover what they are made of.

I think in my heart of hearts that I always wanted to do something like this. So did Jesse. I wanted to live life on the edge, with some danger, all the while helping people who desperately needed it. But ironically FatLand was so stable and cozy that it never gave us that chance. Here, on the Other Side, I see how unstable life is and can be.

I have also learned to value what I had there. At some point, when I get back, I hope to lecture on just how valuable and important it is to maintain FatLand standards and rules. But Fat-Land "rules" are mostly non-rules, statutes that state what people shouldn't do to each other. Here it is all too clear that statutes serve to tell people what they can do to each other and get away with.

Yesterday I transported a lady who hadn't had what I would consider a decent meal for three years, before she managed to get to GymNotTrim. People told her that GymNotTrim charged $300 a day, or something like that. Insane. Probably Winston Stark's propaganda. She and I stopped at another GymNotTrim along the way and had ice cream sundaes—small ones, but definitely tasty. That's one of the ways that Sandor manages to get away with keeping GymNotTrim "legal." He can claim that he serves very small servings of everything in keeping with the Pro-Health Rules and the Non-Approved Food laws and taxes. But if someone wants two of something, they just pay for it. No questions asked.

I think the lady got high on the sundae. She started to tell me about her childhood in a place called Sunderland Bay. She didn't even name the state. She just talked about how happy they were, and how no one even thought to refuse them food or second helpings. "For goodness' sake," she said. "We were kids. Kids need nourishment and fun to grow up happy and healthy. And love. When my granny made her iced oatmeal raisin cookies on Sundays, that was love. She let us all put on the icing and lick the spoon. I shudder when I think of how many experiences the Pro-Health Laws have robbed kids of. And of love."

"The people who pushed through the Pro-Health Laws don't care about happiness and love," I said. "They care about telling people what to do so they can make money. Ease and happiness and love are not part of their vocabulary."

But she definitely inspired me. As I keep thinking about that lady, it makes me even more certain that I and my sister and fellow transporters are doing the right thing. Even if we're arrested.

I know Mira, who is really amazing, by the way, told us how to handle things, and what we're supposed to say. But I would love to simply say to them, "Why don't you arrest the murderers who pushed through the Pro-Health Laws? They're the ones who murdered people and their autonomy and happiness."

I hope both of you are well, Dad and Mom. And I hope Aimee will find happiness in what she is doing.

Love,
Your Daughter Jenna

"I FEEL AS IF MY SENSES are on overload," Aimee said the next morning as they breakfasted on fresh pita bread, damietta cheese and honey. Fresh big dates and figs sat on blue and red plates next to the white porcelain pots with azure flowered trim that held hot coffee.

They were in the Lord Finlay hotel in Alexandria, Egypt. Aimee noticed almost idly that some of the women in the lobby were in brocade veils with lace trim, but others were in jeans. Some were fat, some were thin, some were in-between.

"She loved this place," Ava said. "She came here a lot, to Alexandria, and walked on the Corniche. We'll do that later. Then we'll go to her village."

"You're going to write the article afterwards?"

"Yes. Aimee, journalism—writing articles—is as important as being heroic. Maybe even more so, because how would the world know about heroism if we didn't write about it?"

Aimee sighed. "I could stay here forever. And write." She looked around the bright breakfast room as sun poured onto the blue-branched rug.

Ava laughed. "It is wonderful, isn't it? But there are so many other places you should see first."

"They don't seem to care here," Aimee said. "If you're fat, you're fat.

If you're thin, you're thin. In FatLand, it's more as if you're consciously free. But here, they just live."

"In the not too distant future, you'll see how it is to be in other places," Ava said. She noted with some amusement and approval that a tall, strong-looking man of about thirty was regarding Aimee with undisguised pleasure.

"Are they expecting us in the village?" Aimee asked.

"Oh, yes."

The FatLand Free News
May 2

WHERE SHE CAME FROM:
LEARNING ABOUT AMIYAH
By Ava Bryer & Aimee Johnston

ABU SITYA—THE VILLAGE IS GREEN AND MARSHY, lush in the places where it runs up to the Nile. The fields are brown and green where the sand has been touched by irrigation, but a light baked gold where the sun beats down on them and crusts them until rain or the next flooding cycle catches up with them.

Abu Sitya is not a rich village. People have been dragging crops from these fields from before recorded time. Yet somehow people don't look angry or sad. Even the donkeys who turn the water wheels wear a look of philosophical repose on their sun-worked faces.

Latifah, who sells fish and pulses at the market every Wednesday, beats flour with mortar and pestle. Ground fine, it will become pita bread as it bakes in a clay oven outside her small mud house.

"No one hates anyone here," she says. "We all just want to feed and clothe ourselves and make our lives peaceful for ourselves and our children and their children."

Of course she is speaking through an interpreter. He has been assigned to us by the tourist office in Cairo. I hope that he is translating accurately and ask my next question. "Did you know Amiyah, the dancer?"

She smiles, showing two gaps in her teeth. Then she looks sad. "We all knew her. We all cried when we heard what happened. The person who did that must have carried so much evil in him. She was such a lovely girl."

"Did people here approve of her dancing?"

"They didn't approve or disapprove. They thought that if she could go to Cairo and America, she was doing well. They thought she would live an easier life than we have here."

"Did anyone ever say things about her figure, how she was built?"

Latifah laughs. "The men used to say things. They used to talk about what they would do if they would get her into their beds."

"So they really liked how she was built?"

"Liked? They had dreams about her."

"What was she like when she was young?"

"She was beautiful then, too. She was always singing and dancing. We thought that she might become a famous singer, like Um Kulthoum. But then she started to like dancing more."

"Her parents didn't mind that she sang and danced?"

"She was raised by her grandparents and her mother. Her father died when she was young."

"Did she have any sisters or brothers?"

"Only one sister."

"But if she had had brothers or a father, do you think they would have objected to her dancing?"

"Maybe not, if they thought she could get rich."

"Is her sister still alive?"

"The sister lives in Cairo. She teaches there."

"She is married?"

"Yes."

THERE IS A COFFEEHOUSE at the north end of the village. Several men are seated there when we come in. One is smoking the hookah, the long water pipe. Two are drinking coffee. Two are playing *sheshbesh*, backgammon.

The interpreter offers them our *salaams* and tells them that we are writing about Amiyah. Instantly the mood changes to sadness.

One man says, "She should have never gone there, to America. She should have stayed here, in Egypt."

"To do what?" the man next to him says. "The cafes are not allowed to have dancing girls. In Alexandria, some do in the hotels. But then the girls become prostitutes. That is a shame and a sin."

"But she died there," the first man says. "That was a worse sin. Have the police caught the one who killed her?"

We say through the interpreter that several people were caught, but none punished because the people who planned a lot of the murder escaped to different countries.

"It is horrible," he says. "Give them up to us. We will give them what they deserve."

"You all liked her?" I say.

"We loved her," the second man says. "She had no enemies here. We all wanted her to do well. She was such a happy little girl. And she was so beautiful. That someone could even think of killing her is a crime against Allah."

When we are out of the coffeehouse and on the road once more, back to Cairo, I wonder if Amiyah would still be alive if she were in the village, or in Cairo. But there are those among us who were not meant to stay in one place. And Amiyah gloried in her dancing and in the pleasure it brought to others.

As FatLand did, her village honored her for her beauty and talent and wished only the best for her.

Chapter 21

Margaret

MARGARET STRETCHED and yawned. It was 6 AM, the sun was rising, and she was thirsty and would be hungry soon. Most important, the first run to the House would be completed at 6:30 AM, and there would be people to feed and hide.

"Dave, dear," she whispered, "some green tea would be good. With a bagel and cream cheese. We'll have a better breakfast later, with the folks we greet from the run."

Dave stretched, yawned, and padded out of the room.

Margaret dived into the stall shower in the dressing room, emerged refreshed, and yanked on the denim skirt and white shirt she wore to greet the people rescued on the runs and their rescuers. She looked at the clock. Ten minutes.

She put on shoes and makeup. Twenty minutes. She picked up the intercom to check if Dave had gone to the kitchen.

It was dead.

Oh Lord, she grumbled to herself. *Of all times for things to go down.* She stood up and was about to go down to the kitchen when the door opened. Winston Stark walked into the room.

"You're looking very well, indeed," he said, shutting the door behind him.

"When did you get back?" she said, trying to remain as calm as she could.

"An hour or so ago."

"But you're wanted for a lot of things in this state and probably the country. Won't they—?"

"They can't tell where I am," he said. "Thanks to your putting this house under anti-radar cloud cover."

"Nice to see you," Margaret said. "How long do you intend to stay?"

"Forever."

"Oh, really," Margaret said. "In this house?"

"Exactly. Everything I want is here."

"Including your latest wife?"

"She's somewhere in Austria swimming. Or skiing. Doesn't matter really."

"Won't she sort of wake up one morning and realize you're gone?"

"She might. Then again, she might not. There's a hot new instructor in that resort. Maybe she's busy with him already."

"Has she done that before?"

"Get busy with ski instructors? I have no idea."

"For someone who married her," Margaret said severely, "you seem to have very little idea as to her whereabouts or tendencies."

"Which suits me fine. Or should I say, suited."

"Why the change?"

Winston regarded her. "Oh come now, Margaret, you're not an innocent damsel. Although in what you're wearing, you rather look like one." He sat down on the bed.

With one flick of a button hidden on a podphone in his pocket, he reactivated the intercom. "Safety device," he said. "In case the house was taken over or being subverted from outside."

"Ingenious," Margaret remarked.

Winston picked up the intercom. "Ally, make that two bagels with cream cheese and two green teas. Buffet breakfast later in the Sky Room."

"We usually greet them in the Colorado Room," Margaret said.

"I think they'll have to wait today," Winston said and stretched out on the bed. "We're going to have a little discussion first."

"Oh, really," Margaret said. "And what is it that we are going to discuss?"

"You. Me. Us. The state of the world. Living. Dying. Happiness. Unhappiness."

"For someone who just took a long flight, you are amazingly verbal," Margaret said sternly.

"It's one of my talents," Winston said. He beckoned to her. "Come sit here. I won't eat you. Not yet, anyway."

"I question that," Margaret said. She sat down on the other side of the bed.

Winston laughed. "Good enough for now."

The tea and bagels came. "What did you do with Dave?" she asked as the door shut again.

"Do with him? Nothing. He's busy reorienting the Network Room. Just a few small changes."

"I see," Margaret said, wondering how best to find out how much Stark knew.

"You've been a rather naughty girl," Winston remarked, biting into his bagel. "But you fought really really hard for your cause. I admire that."

"Thanks," Margaret said, biting into her bagel.

"Of course you'll have to retire now."

"From what?"

"From running this house as a Safe House."

"It was due to be changed anyway," Margaret said. "We couldn't keep it much longer."

"Wise policy," Winston said.

"But I do not plan to retire from editing."

"That, my dear Margaret, remains to be seen." Winston locked the door.

"You cannot mean that I would simply live to service you or some such nonsense?" Margaret said.

"I mean," Winston said, "that you look absolutely fetching in that skirt and shirt. So much so that I would like to get you out of it."

"For someone who has so many business concerns, why do you always seem to think about sex three quarters of the time?"

Winston laughed. "To me, business is sexy too."

"FOR A MAN WHO FOUGHT tooth and nail against GymNotTrim since Sandor decided not to associate with you, you seem to have rather an accepting attitude toward fat people," Margaret remarked a few hours later from under the covers.

"I love fat people," Winston said. "Fat women, especially. I love you, actually. That makes me love fat women and fat people. But you kept eluding and evading me, Margaret. I decided for that reason that GymNotTrim had to go. But alas, it is stronger than ever, and growing. I'll have to find some other way to recoup my losses. I think I'll sell Complete Fitness and invest in something else."

"Like what?"

"FatLand."

"What?"

"Oh, come on, Margaret, your infrastructure needs all kinds of help. Bridges, water system, electrical system, even podsystems. I might even start another newspaper there."

"And you think that after everything that has happened, they'll let you waltz in and begin investing. Just like that."

"They might or might not," Stark conceded. Then he smiled.

"You'll try to split the Board, won't you?" Margaret said, wondering if her podmail would still work.

"I won't need to try," he said. "And don't think for a minute that I'd let you podmail my plans all over FatLand. Your device is now disabled."

"I should have known that you would never change."

"I don't," Stark said. "Except in one way. I'm sick of the bimbos and the young clones. I want you. I always have. And I realize now that I want you for all time."

"Very flattering," Margaret said.

"You don't believe me."

"As you said, you don't change. I find it difficult to believe that you would change even in this respect."

Stark sighed. "What can I do to prove it to you? Besides reenabling your pod, that is."

Margaret laughed. "Why do you keep reminding me of the old song from the 1990s about a guy who never changes and keeps wanting his woman friend to keep responding and making all the moves?"

"Margaret, I'll do anything."

She had a sudden thought. Acting subdued, looking down at her own feet, she said, "Let me keep writing. That is all I ask."

"Of course," Stark agreed.

From the Rockies

by Margaret Clancy

So simple, to let the scenery lull you into acquiescence with fate and almost everything else. It snows late here, sometimes into June, but you feel as if you're on top of the world and even creation.

People who frequent the nearby mountains are dressed ultra-fashionably. Often they confine themselves to one hot chocolate per day, one Irish coffee per weekend. The Pro-Health Laws enforcers do not come here. Neither do people interested in promoting size acceptance.

If you stand in certain places at certain times, you can hear the sounds of skiers schussing down a difficult course, the cable cars whizzing overhead, the laughter of children taking it all in and getting high on cold, heights and snow. So easy to pretend that nothing at all exists that is bad, unjust or untoward.

In some ways how easy it is to envy these people their bliss in ignorance, their radioactively bright ski wear, their narrowing of focus to some slopes and a chalet.

And yet how difficult it is to imagine that this confined and protected world will shelter all of these chosen few, all the time.

And when they do learn and have to cope with the fact that there are millions of people a few miles from them who are in prison through no fault of their own, that there are people for whom "fun" is a forbidden quantity, or if they themselves are one day exiled from the frost-encircled paradise of the slopes—what then?

Will they gather enough courage and fortitude to act on their shattering and horrific discoveries? Or will they try to find another paradise—frozen or unfrozen—into which they can vanish?

Immediately upon seeing Margaret's piece in *The FatLand News,* Jenna podphoned Dara. "You saw the third from the last line? 'Frost-encircled paradise.' That's the phrase."

"Yes," Dara said. "That's the one. Time to get the helicopter. She'll go to the roof. We're to circle three times if necessary."

Dara and Sandor left an hour later. "At least my experience in FatLand HeliCorps comes in handy," Sandor said. He banked the helicopter over a couple of mountains, then headed for the coordinates

Jenna gave. "We're not supposed to see anything. They may still have the house under cover."

"Hey, look," Dara said. "Red. I think it's a scarf sticking out over the roof of the house or something. I can even see it from here. Margaret said she would be wearing it."

"Bravo, Margaret," Sandor said, jubilant. They edged down to where the red scarf seemed to be flying.

"We'll get you," Dara yelled as loudly as she could. "Hang on. Can you climb the ladder?"

"She can't hear you from here," Sandor warned.

The helicopter hovered. Suddenly the house started to reveal itself.

"I guess Stark's artificial cloud cover is disappearing," Dara said.

"He's changing the reorientation settings," Sandor said.

"Can you hang on?" Dara yelled down to Margaret.

"You may not have that option," Margaret screamed up to them, not hearing. "Just go!"

But Sandor slowed the speed to one-third while he eased the helicopter down to the roof. Suddenly two helicopters rent the airspace in the distance and began speeding toward them.

"Go!" Margaret yelled.

Disobeying her commmand, Sandor pushed the helicopter door open and grabbed Margaret, pulling her inside.

"Thank God," Dara said. The two women hugged.

Sandor gunned the throttle, banked steeply and sped toward the FatLand border. The two other helicopters advanced on their smaller one and started to fire. Just as they were about to enter FatLand airspace, the FatLand helicopter shuddered and started to plummet. They smelled smoke.

"Fuel," Sandor said tersely. "I think they hit the tank."

"Get out of here," Margaret screamed. "Use your chutes!"

"We've got enough for everyone," Dara said, handing Margaret a chute. She and Sandor were already wearing theirs.

"I can't do this," Margaret said as Dara snapped her chute and prepared to push her out. "I hate heights."

"You want to go back to Stark's castle?" Dara said. "Or burn up when the copter hits the ground?"

"God, no." Margaret held her breath, closed her eyes, and jumped.

Her chute opened at about 3,000 feet and carried her just inside the FatLand border.

Dara's chute opened later, at 2,000 feet, and took her to the Other Side. Margaret heard a police siren erupt.

There was a explosion in the distance. Black smoke whirled through the trees deeper within FatLand. Margaret podphoned Sandor and was relieved when he eventually answered.

There was no response from Dara.

"We have to get her out," she told Sandor.

"I'll go back in," Sandor said.

"With all those police sniffing around, you'd be toast."

"I'm going back," he repeated.

"Not now," Margaret said. "We'll form a rescue effort with FatAnd-Proud. At least we've got to find out where she is and if she's been taken."

And if she's alive, Sandor thought, his heart thudding, his head throbbing dully.

Margaret took a few breaths, then podphoned Alvin, Reevie, Ed, and Joann. Four hours later, exhausted and bruised, communicating by podphone to confirm their locations, she and Sandor arrived at the FatLand Eastern Border Checkpoint.

Chapter 22

Dara

DARA WATCHED AS EACH PRO-HEALTH LAW VIOLATOR was weighed, their weights and Body Mass Index shouted out, and their daily Recommended Caloric Intake recorded on charts and announced.

"Andrew Gilbert: Weight 180. BMI 30. RCI 1200."

"Mella Dawson: Weight 220. BMI 32. RCI 1000."

When they came to her, she said, "First of all, I am not a violator of the Pro-Health Laws since I am not a citizen of the USA. I am a physician from FatLand. Whatever charge you have made against me should be announced."

As she hoped, this embarrassed the Re-education Center workers. "What do we do with her?" one said to the other. "Get a supervisor here."

As they seated her in a chair at the end of the holding area, she said loudly, "Are you aware that putting people on diets of any kind, including restricting their caloric intake, causes them to regain the weight?"

"But we don't let them regain," one worker said. "If they start to regain, we lower the caloric allotment."

"Even if they regain at, say, 500 calories per day?"

The workers all looked embarrassed again. "Look, miss," another said. "We're just doing our jobs."

"Your jobs are to starve people?"

"We're supposed to make sure that they will not get heart attacks or diabetes."

"And what about the thin people who have heart attacks or diabetes?"

They turned away.

The supervisor came about an hour later. She asked what the problem was. The workers told her thar Dara was not a citizen of the USA, and thus was not subject to the Pro-Health Laws.

"Where is she from?" the supervisor asked.

"FatLand."

The supervisor sighed. "We've never gotten one of those. I'll have to podphone the State."

"But until they rule, what do we do?"

The supervisor looked at Dara."Hell if I know. What does she do?"

"Physician."

"Well, ask her to design her own diet, then. But tell her she has to stay more or less within prison bounds. No more than 1500 per day. And if she could keep it a little less, that would be good."

Podmail from Dara Goldenberg to Margaret Clancy

Margaret, I'm here in Colorado Pro-Health Re-education Center #4, Medium Security Division, where a lot of the Pro-Health Law violators are staying.

There is at least a good possibility that they will send me someplace else once they learn what I have done and who I am. Since I am not a Pro-Health Law violator, but a seditious inciter instead, I will probably be sent to a maximum security facility.

People here do not say or hear good things about this facility. So far, though, they seem in no hurry to send me anyplace. The supervisor seems fairly nice, even sympathetic (I keep wondering if she could be one of FatAndProud's underground people, but then I figure that would be simply too farfetched). She let me design my own diet, within the bounds of the 1500 calorie maximum. Of course I also have to abide by the proscriptions of the Pro-Health Laws.

I share a compartment (they don't say "cell" here) with three female Pro-Health Law violators. One was caught storing Twinkies (her terminally ill three year old son liked them. By the way, he was sent to a state institution when she was arrested). One woman was accused of having too much cheese in her diet, some of it black market cheese. The third one had a chocolate craving and tried to evade the Non-Approved Food taxes.

Of course chocolate is forbidden in prison here. They say that rich people somehow manage to smuggle it in. Some organized crime people charge a fortune for it and make a tidy sum.

The scary stuff we hear concerns the maximum security facility where I could conceivably be sent. The maximum there is 1000 calories per day! That frightens me. I think their policy there is simply to starve people into submission. But then the guards play this sadistic game at night. They drop food into the cells and watch the prisoners fight for it.

Oddly enough we are not forbidden from cooking here. Sometimes we sort of put our meals together and add an egg or two. They haven't forbidden eggs yet. Since the supervisor trusts me to come up with the correct calorie count, I simply add the two eggs in and divide the count by four. How ironic, that when we were required to study this stuff in FatLand Medical School in one course only, I simply forgot most of it. Now I have had to refresh myself thoroughly, mostly with the help of my compartment mates.

We are also supposed to have daily exercise periods. For some reason they have stopped them lately. Mostly women walk around the yard after lunch. Probably better than organized exercise, and they get to talk to people. I've actually met a writer, someone known to FatAndProud, and a sculptor—one who used to like to create sculptures of full-figured women's bodies, as they call them here. Her sculptures were starting to become quite popular just when the Pro-Health Laws were passed.

Podmail from Sandor Forman to Dara Goldenberg

Oh, babe.

I feel so torn up. I feel as if I want to run in there and kidnap you, as you arranged to have done for me. But people tell me you're doing an amazing job by being the first person to be able to tell us firsthand what goes on in the Re-education Center prisons on the Other Side, with people who have supposedly violated the Pro-Health Laws.

But I cannot stand the thought of your being sent to a maximum security prison there. I am sure it would be interesting and perhaps useful to have your account of the proceedings, but I don't think I'd be able to stand by and watch.

So, consider this an order, even though we have not given each other orders before. THE MINUTE YOU FIND OUT YOU ARE BEING TRANSFERRED, YOU PODMAIL ONE OF US. DO YOU HEAR ME? THE MINUTE YOU FIND OUT. NOT ONE SECOND LATER.

And yeah, we hear that the Anti-Diet revolution is starting to ignite there. The most amazing part of it is that we are now getting requests from ten to fifteen towns or even cities per day about starting Anti-Diet Zones after they see our new website. It is as if Jesse is redeeming himself in death for the terrible thing he took part in in life. Soon most of the Other Side will be a series of Anti-Diet Zones, and the Pro-Health Laws will be effectively circumvented.

But my darling, please please remember. The minute you learn that you are being transferred, PODMAIL OR CALL. NOT ONE SECOND LATER.

Don't leave me alone. It is already like hell. I cannot imagine being without you much longer.

Much Love,

Sandor

PODMAIL FROM DARA GOLDENBERG TO SANDOR FORMAN

Okay, Sandor, here it is, officially.

I think they really wanted to keep me here. The supervisor especially seemed to like me, and so did my compartment mates. But orders came down from the State Pro-Health department a couple of hours ago. They are sending a prison transport for me and four others. Since these other four are Pro-Health violators, goodness knows what they have done to wind up in maximum security.

I am scared, but sort of interested. I will podmail again upon arrival, since I think they take our pods away from us when we get there.

PODMAIL #2 FROM DARA GOLDENBERG TO SANDOR FORMAN

This is strange. They have stopped the truck. They are taking us out. Somehow I don't like the look of this. If I can get out of the line, I am going to escape.

PODMAIL FROM SANDOR FORMAN TO MARGARET CLANCY, ALVIN JOHNSON, REEVIE JOHNSON, ED TORELLI, JOANN TORELLI

Is the helicopter ready?

PODMAIL FROM MARGARET CLANCY TO SANDOR FORMAN

Am ordering it out now. Do you want to go?

PODMAIL FROM SANDOR FORMAN TO MARGARET CLANCY

Yes.

HALF AN HOUR LATER, one of four helicopters kept ready by the FatLand Board headed out of FatLand airspace into Colorado airspace. As soon as it entered Colorado, its headlights started to scan the highways and offroads used by Colorado prison transport closest to Colorado Re-education Center #4.

Four bodies were located, but Dara's was not among them.

PODMAIL FROM MARGARET CLANCY
TO SANDOR FORMAN

We'll keep looking, Sandor. I promise.

PODMAIL FROM SANDOR FORMAN
TO MARGARET CLANCY

I'll keep looking. Whatever it takes.

TWO DAYS LATER, a podmail containing a heading but no message
was received from Dara.
"At least she's out there somewhere!" Sandor exulted to the Board,
who had convened an emergency meeting.
"Could also mean her pod was programmed to do that," Ed commented. "But still—maybe she's okay after all."

PODMAIL FROM MIRA TORELLI
TO JOANN TORELLI

In answer to your Board's podmail, we have not heard or seen
anything of Dara Goldenberg. We did hear about the shooting
you mention. We will send FatAndProud members to scour the
area.

I miss you all.

In Fat Acceptance Solidarity,
Mira

PODMAIL FROM SANDOR FORMAN
TO MARGARET CLANCY

She's out there somewhere. I know she is.

THE HELICOPTER SWOOPED DOWN without warning.
"Get in, lassie," Drew Harris said to Dara, who was lying in a field

of tall grass, her ear to the ground. "Don't want the meanies to get you, now, do we?"

"Do I have a choice?"

"Not really," Winston Stark said.

Supported on either side by Harris and Stark, Dara entered the helicopter. Stark pressed a chocolate croissant into her hand. "Greetings," he said.

"Where are you taking me?"

"I think you know," Harris said. "Gets to be fun, rescuing you guys."

"Holding me for ransom?"

"Something like that," Harris agreed.

"Oh well," Dara sighed. "I guess you're good at that by now."

"Your pod, please," Harris said.

Reluctantly Dara handed him the pod. "Good," Harris said. "Now let's talk."

Podmail from Drew Harris to the members of the Board of FatLand

Call off your hounds. She's alive. We have her. We will negotiate with Sandor.

Podmail from Sandor Forman to Drew Harris

Sure. Where and when?

Podmail from Drew Harris to Sandor Forman

Here. As soon as possible.

"You know about the system in the house now," Margaret said as Sandor boarded a FatLand helicopter. "But don't raise the covering until you disable the alarms."

"Will do," Sandor said. He shook hands with the Board members. "Thanks for everything."

"Here's hoping it works," Reevie said.

"Go with all our blessings and get back with her soon," Alvin said.

"Stay safe," Ed said.

"Come back soon," Joann said.

They watched as the helicopter started up, rose and wafted off into the distance. Taking comfort in each other's company, they headed back to the van, which was spacious and held their strong fat bodies without any cramping.

Chapter 23

Aimee & Ava

AVA ZIPPED THE LAST BAG shut. "Have fun," she said to Aimee. "And remember, don't stay out until after 11 PM alone."

"You have fun, too," Aimee said, getting off the bed. She took Ava's hand and squeezed it.

"I will. I hope Sandor finds Dara and is able to get her out of there."

"At least she's alive and well and not too uncomfortable."

"For now," Ava agreed. "What should I buy you from Greece?"

"Sandals," Aimee said. "I like the ones here, but I want to get a pair from each country."

"Done."

After Ava left, Aimee opened the blinds and stared out at Cairo. She picked out different traffic patterns on different streets, all completely snarled. Not being able to think of anything constructive to do immediately, she decided to go down to lunch.

The waiter smiled at her. "Nice to see you," he said, and handed her a menu.

"*Shukran,*" Aimee said.

The waiter's smile became a beam. "Very good."

A man in his early thirties wearing a navy suit, white shirt, and tie walked in. He saw the waiter and caught his eye. "I will be back," the waiter said. "You take your time, order something very tasty."

The waiter came back. "Miss, Abboud is asking if he can sit with you."

"Why not?" Aimee said. "It's more friendly that way."

The waiter seated Abboud across from Aimee, bowed, then left.

Abboud's skin, Aimee decided, was the color of a nutmeg with sun on it. His smile spread into his dark, dark eyes. "In your white dress," he said to her, "you look like a goddess."

I think my life is beginning, Aimee thought. *Or beginning again.* She said, "In that case, you may order for us."

"It will be my pleasure," Abboud said.

REFLECTIONS IN MID-REVOLUTION, FROM GREECE
BY AVA BRYER
SPECIAL TO *The FatLand Free News*

I AM IN ATHENS NOW.

Every night as light shines from the young moon, I dance my way up as close as I can to the deeper light of a monument, a celebration that has existed here for thousands of years. Well, as close as I can the building is undergoing an extensive renovation right now. As if one could renovate a temple of millennia. But from what I have been told, the building would crumble if "emergency measures" were not taken.

During the day I simply walk. Sometimes I buy a few things feta cheese, savory salty olives, incomparable pine nuts, Greek pickled beets, salad with anchovies and hard-cooked eggs from a taverna where they serve those amazing Greek white table wines that seem to make every meal a festival.

And then, amid my temporary sense of contentment, I remember why I am halfway across the world, and also that someone who was so dear to me cannot savor the salty olives or nuts or cheese. And then the pain stops me mid-step or mid-sentence.

There seems to be no simple answer to why Amiyah died. It involves greed, desperation, anger and ignorance. But those lofty nouns do not seem to communicate just what it was that drove a group of people to place under the car she was renting the device that killed her. There are so many little pieces to the puzzle.

I hoped that I would perhaps pick up a few of the pieces in Egypt, where she was born and lived almost all of her life. But all I kept coming up with is that her life there, sunny and exuberant by all accounts, seemed to have nothing to do with what happened to her in FatLand.

Sometimes I did sense her in the hot earth, the tempered sky, the ageless mud brick houses. But she was always smiling and dancing. Perhaps this in itself is the way she would have wanted us to remember her.

Now, as my traveling companion discovers how much she likes staying in Egypt, where Amiyah was from, it occurs to me that somehow Amiyah is blessing her, if that can be, with her own *joie-de-vivre*, her sensual, sensuous, spontaneous appreciation of life and body and the myriad sensations waiting just this side of discovery for anyone who is young enough at heart to feel them.

And I feel a little less sad and guilty for dancing in the light of the Parthenon.

As I WRITE THIS IN GREECE, a revolution is taking place in the United States of America. People are finally deciding that they do not need others to tell them what to put and what not to put in their mouths and bodies. Somehow this too, in so many ways, seems to be what Amiyah would celebrate and bless.

Beautiful fat Amiyah thought it was laughable, although in a sad way, how medical—and non-medical—experts and pundits of every stripe somehow strove to diminish people—especially women—robbing them of control and self-esteem as they told them what they could and could not put in their mouths.

This trend reached an extreme in the Pro-Health Laws, which are finally being nullified even as I write, as people all over the USA set up Diet-Free Zones. But how much suffering, how much bloodshed, how many tears and how much sickness had to occur before people woke up to the fact that food restriction and forced starvation bring nothing but pain and suffering and decreased life spans to those who undergo them?

FatLand is playing a major role in this revolution as it attempts to implement what we FatLanders have known for so many years that depriving people of anything, including food, leads not to health but to sickness.

Here in Greece, as I open a jar of pickled beets and slosh olive oil and vinegar onto a bed of greens, feta cheese, and pine nuts, and add some anchovies, I know that Amiyah wholeheartedly approved of what we did and how we live, just as she would approve our helping our friends on the Other Side in their time of great need and heroism.

Rest happy, Amiyah. Your light is with us.

Chapter 24

Jenna

JENNA STEERED THE VEHICLE slowly, waiting until the search-lights slanted to another part of the checkpoint.

"Don't worry," she said to the frightened Coloradoans she was trans-porting. They had managed to escape from Prison #5, a maximum security facility for those who had not only violated the Pro-Health Laws, but had incited others to violate them, according to the statute. "You'll be safe soon."

Jenna stopped the vehicle when it was in front of the checkpoint. She reached into the insulated silver bag and brought out a cherry pie with whipped cream. As per instructions, she brought out a torch and heated the area slightly so the smell of the pie would waft around the van.

"Wow," the guard said. "Got something pretty aromatic there." He sniffed. "Everyone have papers?"

Jenna handed the guard her papers and those of the two escaping prisoners. "High school reunion," she said.

"Nice." The guard took the papers and scrutinized them. Jenna held her breath. This was when she would have to gun the brake or ease out, depending on the attitude of the guard and if he recognized the two escapees from the posters on the walls. But these days there were so many escapees that it was difficult even for the guards to recall every one of them. Jenna was counting on that, as well.

"Look," she said, gesturing to the cherry pie. "We have a few of these. A gift. Would you like to have this one?"

"Well," the guard said, peering at the pie with huge eyes, "I can't say

I'd mind."

What was good about this procedure, Jenna knew, was that if a guard accepted a pie once, he was even more likely to accept a pie the next time. She wrote his name very quickly in her phonecorder, then handed the pie to him. "Be very careful," she cautioned in her friendliest voice. "It has whipped cream on top."

"Oh, I know," the guard said, taking the pie and feasting his eyes on it almost literally. "Have a safe trip, folks."

"Thanks," Jenna said as she eased through the checkpoint.

The two former prisoners breathed deeply as they came to the "Welcome to FatLand" sign.

"Yep," Jenna said. "We're here."

"Thank goodness," the woman said.

The van rolled up to the gate. "Howdy," the FatLand guard said to Jenna. "Glad to see you."

"Glad to see you, too," Jenna said.

Part IV

Season of Hope

DEAR FATLAND BOARD,

We wish to thank you for your help and guidance.

We would like to inform you that as of today, our proud city of Ann Arbor, Michigan is now diet-free. As per the recommendations of your site, we have adopted the following rules.

- There shall be no discussion of weight whatsoever in any public place or arena. This includes any place that does not constitute the private domicile of any citizen.

- There shall be no weight scales in any facility, whether medical or other.

- No person shall be forced to exercise or reduce food intake at any time. Any instance of forced exercise or reduced food intake shall constitute an indictable offense.

- Any material on video or electronic media discussing weight shall be censored or banned.

- Any person who discusses or mentions the weight of another shall be indicted if the person whose weight was discussed or mentions wishes to bring charges against the person who discussed or mentioned her or his weight.

- Any discrimination by any concern or corporation, public or private, in the field of hiring shall constitute grounds for indictment of the individuals involved or the entire concern or corporation.

We hereby name Ann Arbor, Michigan a Size Acceptance Zone. All people of all sizes are welcome to live and work here without experiencing harassment and discrimination because of their sizes.

To The Board of FatLand:

We wish to inform you that we, the people of the proud State of Tennessee, have voted to make the entire state a No-Diet Zone...

To the FatLand Board:

We are pleased to tell you that we of the beautiful state of Hawaii have voted to make our state a No-Diet zone...

To the Board:

We hereby commend you for your help in the matter of subverting and nullifying the Pro-Health Laws. We have voted to make our city—Grand Forks, North Dakota—a No-Diet Zone.

To the Folks of the FatLand Board:

Howdy. The City of Austin, Texas hereby declares itself a No-Diet Zone.

To the Board:

The County of the Bronx, New York is now a No-Diet Zone...

To the FatLand Board:

We are pleased to announce that the city and incorporated areas of Madison, Wisconsin now constitute a No-Diet Zone. Man, triple-taxing our beer and cheese pretzels and fried fish and cheese fries and homemade ice cream was the pits! Our cows are celebrating by running over the Common...Here are ten coupons for cheese fries on us.

To the Board:

We can't thank you enough. The city of Marblehead, Massachusetts, first in patriotism, first in yachts, and first home of the U.S. Navy, has voted to become a No-Diet Zone…

To the FatLand Board:

We, the great city of San Francisco, salute you for your efforts to take back the nation from the grip of the Pro-Health Laws. We are voting today on a resolution to adopt the statute that will make our city a No-Diet Zone. We expect that it will pass overwhelmingly.

Sometimes certain overzealous elements seem to grab our nation by the throat, almost always in the interest of money and power, as they wrap themselves in the banner of Health or Patriotism or Anti-X or -Y. But once the spark ignites, the people of the USA fight back and take back their individualistic, quirky, eccentric, self-reliant political entities.

Here's to the ignition and combustion…

The End and the Beginning

About the Author

FRANNIE ZELLMAN received her MA in creative writing from Boston University in 1980 and blames none of her professors for what she has done or written since.

SHE IS A MEMBER of the National Association to Advance Fat Acceptance (NAAFA) and has taught writing workshops for people of size. She is the editor of *Fat Poets Speak: Voices of the Fat Poets' Society*, also published by Pearlsong Press. She remains an active member of the Fat Poets' Society and has recently started an online fiction writing group called the Fat Fiction Forum.

VISIT FRANNIE ON THE WEB at http://www.fatfrannie.wordpress.com.

Excerpt from

FAT POETS SPEAK
VOICES OF THE FAT POETS' SOCIETY
EDITED BY FRANNIE ZELLMAN
(2009) Pearlsong Press

I SING THE FAT SELF
(To the memory of Walt Whitman)

I sing the fat self that flourishes, acquires girth,
births and blooms its stomach and thighs and limbs,
soft but sturdy as it flows among people and
things it knows and greets. I sing the self that bounces,
plump and easy and free, not tightened or wired
or cut like meat into the correct sizes for freezing and eating. I
sing the self that hugs and is hugged, is cuddled in all places,
sleeps and slips sweetly against its loving partners, limned
by colors fine and bright, limbed in lace and silk and cotton
to flower its curves and cleavage and comeliness.

I sing the fat self that thumps with a great triumphant splash
into creeks, rivers, lakes and oceans, spraying eddies
and currents and waves as the water sloshes over its luscious
wealth of skin and muscle and heft. I sing the self
that rends the air as it spills up to balance a serve, aims clear,
smacks, spikes and volleys and digs the ground,
its strong fat haunches planted sleek and fast as it
passes to players, then bounds up and anchors the net. I
sing the self that runs newly-dried turf, fit, fat and swinging
from base to base after batting over heads and hands and heaps
of scrambling fans.

I sing the fat self that sows, rends, reaps, harvests, mulling each
seed and petal and plant it worked into earth wetted and
mulched and mowed into wide waiting warmth. I sing the self
that once molded, still molds clay into loving fat women with
plentiful breasts and hips and thighs and
furred organs of pleasure.

I sing the fat self that wells into city streets, its arms akimbo
with briefcase and cellphone and printouts of stately, high,
thick buildings yet to be born. I sing the self that struts
high on scaffolds after welding metal and glass into
windows and rafters and beams and partitions, its muscled
arms and strong, succulent chest pointing to where the
next fire will take wood and make of it a tower.

I sing the fat self that feeds its lovely fat children and their
friends, that hugs its plump grandmother with her soft
cheeks and gently knowing hands. I sing the self that
argues for its right to stay fat and free, the self that celebrates
growth, nurturing, strength, fullness, roundness. I sing the self
that raises its voice for all who are spurned,
hated, disliked, ostracized, ignored.

I sing the fat soul.

FRANNIE ZELLMAN

About Pearlsong Press

PEARLSONG PRESS is an independent publishing company dedicated to providing books and resources that entertain while expanding perspectives on the self and the world. The company was founded by Peggy Elam, Ph.D., a psychologist and journalist, in 2003.

PEARLS ARE FORMED when a piece of sand or grit or other abrasive, annoying, or even dangerous substance enters an oyster and triggers its protective response. The substance is coated with shimmering opalescent nacre ("mother of pearl"), the coats eventually building up to produce a beautiful gem. The self-healing response of the oyster thus transforms suffering into a thing of beauty.

The pearl-creating process reflects our company's desire to move outside a pathological or "disease" based model into a more integrative and transcendent perspective on life, health, and well-being. A move out of suffering into joy.

And that, we think, is something to sing about.

PEARLSONG PRESS endorses **Health At Every Size**, an approach to health and well-being that celebrates natural diversity in body size and encourages people to stop focusing on weight (or any external measurement) in favor of listening to and respecting natural appetites for food, drink, sleep, rest, movement, and recreation. While not every book we publish specifically promotes Health At Every Size (by, for instance, featuring fat heroines or educating readers on size acceptance), none of our books or other resources will contradict this holistic and body-positive perspective.

WE ENCOURAGE YOU to **enjoy, enlarge, enlighten and enliven yourself** with other Pearlsong Press books and products, which you can purchase at www.pearlsong.com, Amazon.com or your favorite bookstore. Keep up with us through our blog at www.pearlsongpress.com.

Fat Poets Speak: Voices of the Fat Poets' Society
Frannie Zellman, Ed.

The Program : A Novel
by Charlie Lovett

Off Kilter: A Woman's Journey to Peace with Scoliosis,
Her Mother, & Her Polish Heritage
by Linda C. Wisniewski

Splendid Seniors: Great Lives, Great Deeds
by Jack Adler

The Singing of Swans
a novel about the Divine Feminine
by Mary Saracino

Beyond Measure:
A Memoir About Short Stature & Inner Growth
by Ellen Frankel

Unconventional Means:
The Dream Down Under
by Anne Richardson Williams

Taking Up Space:
How Eating Well & Exercising Regularly Changed My Life
by Pattie Thomas, Ph.D.
with Carl Wilkerson, M.B.A.
(foreword by Paul Campos, author of
The Obesity Myth)

Romance novels and short stories
featuring Big Beautiful Heroines
by Pat Ballard, the Queen of Rubenesque Romances:
    The Best Man
    Abigail's Revenge
    Dangerous Curves Ahead
    Wanted: One Groom
    Nobody's Perfect
    His Brother's Child
    A Worthy Heir

& Judy Bagshaw:
    At Long Last, Love: A Collection

& Pat Ballard's *Ten Steps to Loving Your Body*
(No Matter What Size You Are)

Printed in the United States
219550BV00001B/35/P

9 781597 190152